The Rose of Amzharr by Eddie Bar

The Rose of Amzharr

Print edition ISBN: 9798818610559

The Rose of Amzharr

A massive thank you to everyone who has helped get this journey started.

The Rose of Amzharr

Foreword

Lost in folds of darkness, lit by the reflected lights of a thousand stars, a world nestles on the very edge of reality. It is broken. Held together by promises and hope. Great lands border mighty seas. Deep abysses hide within the bellies of mighty mountains. Through them all cuts the Void. The Void is a fog, so thick in places that it can be walked upon, and even tunnelled through. It is in a constant state of flux. There are islands hidden within that have existed for centuries, whilst others come and go in the blinking of an eye. Navigating the Void can be a risky business as the ground can, quite literally, disappear from beneath your feet, leaving only a grey mist and an eternal fall.

The world was broken and tainted by its immortal creators, and their offspring, through their great wars and elaborate schemes. Although many still survive, they have become bored of their once perfect plaything. They cling to it still though, their roots embedded in its very core, their sleepy grasp reaching into every nook of existence, but seldom stirring.

Now they leave the scheming and dreaming to the younger races - those that have the energy and ambition of youth to try again that which has already failed, discover that which has been discarded, and destroy that which is already broken.

Occasionally, the interest of an immortal is piqued by some suggestion, or grand strategy. On those occasions they cast their eyes, and agents, about the world to aid or hinder, often on a whim. But in an existence that lasts an eternity, where a century passes in the blink of an eye, boredom quickly sets in, and they return to watching for the next bauble to break the monotony of a life without end.

The Rose of Amzharr

Chapter 1

An irk sat in the cool canopy of an oak tree, watching a tall lad with broad shoulders, somewhere between his late teens and early twenties, skimming stones across a lake. His brown hair was long and a thick beard hid half of his face. He wore a simple white shirt and pair of trousers, both made from the same worn-out material. The garments were ill-fitting and poorly stitched, made for comfort as opposed to high fashion. The scent of summer jasmine laced the warm afternoon air, making the forest feel fresh and clean. It wasn't the most compelling of sights. The man wasn't particularly good at casting the tiny rocks into the cool, crystal waters, and most simply sank on the first splash to be reunited with their friends from the shore. This, however, was not the kind of afternoon that demanded a reason, compelling or otherwise, to simply be.

The irk's head lazily twitched to one side, a sign of frustration that the man appeared to have spent so many years in this beautiful, blessed enclave, and yet had seemingly failed to achieve anything at all - including the mastery of skimming stones. Almost eighty years had passed since the irk had watched him scrabbling up the hill, over rocks and through the thick thorns that hid the entrance, snarling hounds and angry voices at his heels. The lad, then a boy of no more than twelve summers, had uttered the prayer of sanctuary and the spirits had responded. The Guardian trees had moved to hide him and, faced with a wall of wood that his pursuers could not see a way through, the snarling hounds and angry voices had quickly dissipated.

At the time the irk had been excited by the boy's arrival. It had been many decades, centuries even, since the Guardian trees had last stirred. The boy had uttered words long forgotten, even to the immortals, and in return had received protection granted so very rarely, and never before to a human. The irk took this as a sign of greatness in the child, spending the next five years observing him. He wondered what powers he might have or grow into. But whatever powers or charms the child might have had, the irk eventually conceded, were at best well hidden - so well hidden that eventually the irk lost all interest in him. The child spent his days throwing rocks into the water and eating as much as he could of the food provided to him by the spirits of the grove. So, the irk began to venture out into the world again, returning frequently in the hope that there would be some significant evolution in his absence. If the evolution had ever happened, the irk told himself following each visit in a bid to keep the embers of his own hopes alive, he had not noticed it, and so his visits became fewer and farther between.

There is no easy way to describe irks. If you imagine a human squeezed into a squirrel, visually, you'd be on the right track. They are small, highly energetic, great climbers, talkative and have, for their size, huge bushy tails. They are long-lived, incredibly precocious, and very nosy. All this, combined with their passion for adventure, means they have a near encyclopaedic knowledge of the world, which they are only too happy to share whether asked to or not.

"Eighty years," the irk muttered to himself. "Eighty years and he's barely scraped through puberty. Talk about a disappointment."

He reached out a small paw in a vain attempt to locate a half-eaten nut lying to one side of him, just outside of his peripheral vision, and something suddenly struck him. Because sometimes, no matter how clearly an image is presented to you, it takes a bit of a nudge to really see the whole picture.

"Oh," the irk gasped, taken aback by what had been under his nose for so many years now. "That's not right. Not right at all."

The irk stopped feeling around for his nut and sat bolt upright. He quickly looked around to confirm the position of his snack. Yes, it was odd that a human who must have been around ninety summers old didn't look a day past twenty, but not so odd it warranted losing food over.

He wondered if the lad had realised that he had now outlived most humans by about thirty years. He hoped he had, but given the lad's apparent lack of achievements, including that of simply letting his body age, the irk decided there was a good chance it very well may have escaped his notice. There was, of course, only one way to find out. He scampered around and along a series of branches until he was within shouting distance of the lad.

"You'd have thought after all these years you'd be just a little better at that?" the irk shouted in his high-pitched voice, keeping a branch between them so that he would remain out of sight.

The lad, just about to launch another rock across the pond, stopped and looked around. "What?" he said in a tone that suggested a boredom with his current pursuit, as well as the wider pursuit of existence.

"I'm wondering why, after all these years, the best you can manage is just a couple of skips?" asked the invisible irk.

2

"I did four once," the lad replied, seemingly unperturbed by the ownerless voice, determined to put right the slur levied at him. "Anyway, what's it to you?"

"Just interested," the irk replied genially before adding, "Exactly how old are you?"

Arm already moving, the man launched the rock in his hand. However, what little investment he had in the activity had disappeared the moment the question reached his ears. The stone plopped listlessly into the water some distance from its companions.

"I don't really know," he answered slowly, his initial disinterest in the voice and what it had to say starting to change. "Who are you?"

The man's tone was now loaded with suspicion. He turned towards the trees, taking a step in what he thought was the direction the voice had come from. "What are you doing here?"

"Show yourself," he demanded, suspicion starting to give way to anger.

The irk toyed with the idea of introducing himself, but there was something about the mix of fear, paranoia even, and anger that was growing in the man's voice that suggested they might not immediately hit it off. It was clear that something about what he had said had rattled the lad, and he wondered if there might be an opportunity to provoke some sort of activity in the lazy slob. Deciding that discretion was, for the time being, the better part of valour, the irk withdrew. He returned to his half-eaten nut, interested to see what the lad would do next.

The abrupt silence completed the transformation of fear into paranoia. The man had heard a voice in the forest once before, when he had thought that the sanctuary was a safe place, sealed off from the outside world. That voice had taught him there were far more dangerous things in the world than other humans with hounds and pitchforks. It had taught him nowhere was safe; no matter how hidden, how protected, there was always a way in - old ways, dangerous ways, but ways nonetheless.

He continued to stand, but now he turned erratically on the spot trying to see, or hear, anything that might give away any sign of the owner of the new voice. He waited for more words, but there were none. He wondered what the voice wanted. It didn't sound the same as the one he'd heard before, so many years ago now, still so memorable, and so chilling.

There had been a coldness that had made him shiver. It had pierced his skin and crept into his veins slowing everything down. Each word had hurt him. Each sentence had felt like a jagged blade pulled slowly across his bare skin. Yes, a price had been offered and paid for his services, but his agreement had been extracted.

He had been twenty when the voice had spoken to him. Old enough to be considered a man, but his lonely years in the sanctuary away from the experiences of the world meant he was only a man in years. He still viewed the world beyond with a child's naivety so, despite the pain in the agreement, there was an excitement in the adventure that followed and discovery in the journey. There was even a fleeting moment of time where a return to the sanctuary seemed impossible.

Then the job was done. The fee was in his pocket, and he celebrated until he lay in the warm glow of booze and exhausted flesh. But disappointment comes just as certainly as the morning after the night before. The warm glow turned into a throbbing headache and a sticky mess with a terrifying bill to be paid.

Realisation dawned with the sun, and although there were no angry voices, or snarling hounds, the silence turned out to be far worse. Blood soaked the bed he lay on. Limbs reached out towards him from every direction, yet their owners' heads and torsos were no longer attached to them. He felt something hover at his shoulder. Ethereal talons stretched towards him. Hurriedly he made his escape through a window before the scene could be discovered, and ran for the sanctuary, hoping whatever followed him would not be able to find a way in.

Chapter 2

As daylight faded the lad was still on edge, even though he had heard no more from the voice throughout the rest of the afternoon. He lit a small fire in front of his hut. The hut had been built just a few metres from the lake, on a slight rise. He had no idea who had built it; it had just been there when he had arrived and, despite its basic design, it had served him well enough over the years. He sat with his back against a tree trunk and watched the flames dance wildly as they ate the dried kindling, before settling back to a gentle glow that would eventually die with the day. This was the part of the day he hated the least. Sleep was coming. Sleep took time from him that he would otherwise have to fill, granting him his daily respite from loneliness and boredom.

This evening was different though. He was awake and alert at a time when his eyelids would normally have been heavy, and his body ready for rest. The voice earlier in the day had set his heart racing and sent adrenalin surging through his body, preparing him to either run or fight, although he had a distinct preference for the former. He had tried his best to put it from his mind as dusk settled and a kaleidoscope of pinks and yellows filled the sky, but he couldn't completely erase the feeling that whatever had spoken to him was still out there somewhere, still watching him.

He tried to convince himself that the voice had been conversational, even friendly, but he couldn't move on from the question about his age. And so, rather than quietly falling asleep as the fire burnt itself out, his eyes remained open as darkness finally wrapped itself around the sanctuary. His vision reduced to mere metres, the world around him seemed to change its nature. Every crack and rustle made his pulse race. Eventually, what he hoped was his imagination got the better of him and he ran into the hut. He opened the lid of a small chest that sat at the end of his bed and pulled out a belt. Attached to the belt was a knife in a sheath. Both knife and sheath were well made. A little decoration hinted at the maker's skill as an artist, but did not distract from the nature of the tool. He fumbled in the darkness for the small sharpening stone that had its own compartment at the back of the sheath, before slumping on his bed, drawing the blade, and slowly dragging it across the stone.

"How old are you?"

That's what the voice had asked. Why would it ask that question? Did it already know how old he was? Did it know that despite his youthful looks he had spent more summers in this place than he cared to think about, and far more than he could count? And even though he could barely count at all he knew full well, that whatever the exact number was, it was far in excess of the number of summers any normal human should spend anywhere, except maybe in the world beyond.

He sat in silent contemplation long after the knife was once again sharp and back in its sheath. He stirred only as the first traces of light started to turn black to darkest blue, far away beyond the trees on the other side of the lake.

He stood and walked out of the hut towards the water's edge. The lake dominated most of the sanctuary. The clear waters were a perfect mirror of the sky above, and on this moonless, starless dawn the two seemed to flow into one another. The lad wondered if he were to walk into the water and start swimming whether he would be able to swim into the sky? He threw the thought away, recognising it only too well for what it was: a search for another escape route. Was he really looking for a sanctuary within a sanctuary? An escape from this escape?

He turned over and over in his mind the notion that the world itself hated him. It had, after all, tried twice to rid itself of him. Yet for some reason he was still here. Did that mean he had somehow gained the upper hand? Was he winning? He found it hard to believe that the unproductive years spent at the water edge equated to the life of a winner. Shouldn't there have been more to it than that? He wondered if the years alone were finally taking their toll, and whether madness now stood ready to take him - if it had not taken him years earlier and was only now letting him know.

He walked the well-worn path to the water's edge, each footstep landed on solid brown earth devoid of the long grasses and ferns that lazily overhung it, obscuring it from sight. Dew-laden foliage brushed against his trousers, sharing its burden, and leaving dark patches of damp below his knees. He found the place he had thrown stones from the day before and turned to face the trees. He took a deep breath, and with a rare rush of courage announced to no one in particular, "If you want to talk, talk now... before I get my head around what a bloody stupid idea this is."

The irk allowed a grin to fill his face from ear to ear. He savoured it briefly before replacing it with something a little more appropriate. Even the little creature knew it didn't help to start a conversation like this with a face quite that smug. He had thought that sooner or later the lad's curiosity would get the better of him, although the irk did have to admit to himself he had held out a lot longer than he had expected.

The sun had ventured a little higher into the sky and silhouetted the lad against the slowly lightening blue of the water and aether he stood with his back to. The irk scampered down from the tree he had been waiting in, through the long grass to the shore, and climbed to the top of an upturned log that served the lad equally as a seat or table, depending on his needs.

"Good morning sir, I am Joggle. Might I have the pleasure of your name?" asked the irk enthusiastically, pulling himself up to his full height.

The lad looked at the little creature. His expression went from abject disappointment to a strange mix of embarrassment and relief. He smiled. "An irk. My gods, a sleepless night all for the sake of an irk."

Joggle took immediate exception to being addressed as though he were an irrelevance, like some meagre hamster or guinea pig. However, that the lad knew of his race piqued his interest, and he resisted the instinctive need to deliver a long and informative lecture on the greatness of irks. It reminded him that despite the incredibly low standards he now held the lad to, and considered him to fail on each and every one, there was a deep intrigue that surrounded him. After all, a failure to age correctly, or possibly even at all, is rarely as a result of laziness in humans.

"Correct. I am indeed an irk," Joggle said, puffing his little chest out in an impossible endeavour to seem larger, and more important, than the average hamster. "Might I have the pleasure of your name, young sir?"

"I'm not sure how much of a pleasure my name brings, but you can have it anyway. It's Gerald," the lad mumbled. "What brings you here?"

"Normally the nuts," Joggle replied. "They are quite exquisite, I believe it's something to do with the water. But on my more recent visits I have been increasingly interested in you."

Gerald eyed the irk up and down again, not a time-consuming activity, but this time with a little more suspicion as Joggle's admission had put Gerald on the defensive once more. Joggle's chirpiness annoyed him, and the thought of the little animal observing him like some sort of exhibit irritated him further. But it wasn't just that; there was something else about the creature that was worming away under his skin. Maybe it was because Joggle had a life outside the sanctuary, whilst he wasted his away in the forest that needled him. Maybe it was because his presence reminded him that other things could also come and go as well, things that weren't as harmless as the little irk seemed to be. Or maybe it was both of these possibilities.

"Visits?" Gerald cried. "I thought this place was meant to be a safe haven. A place of protection? Not a bloody town square on market day with people just wandering in and out whenever they bloody well choose."

"Calm down my friend. Nothing is impenetrable," Joggle said, in a way that Gerald could have sworn was intended to be reassuring, whilst raising and lowering his paws in a gesture meant to signal to Gerald that he should relax. "The world is a very old place, and if you know where to look there is a way into everything. Fortunately, I am very old, and so know many ways into many places."

Gerald let the creature's words sink in, and irritation gave way to a much deeper and darker fear, one that he had pushed from his mind and forced into hiding almost seventy years ago. Maybe it was because of the pain the voice had caused him, or the horrific sight of the dismembered bodies in the brothel. Maybe it was the unseen, unheard feeling that had chased him from the city, leaving grasping claw marks across his back and shoulders, but as soon as he had returned to the sanctuary he had done his best to put the whole miserable adventure behind him.

Because of that he had never allowed himself to ask how the voice that had started it all had entered his little world. He chose instead to avoid the questions that would likely result in him asking whether whatever had chased him back to his hut by the lake might also find a way in. In retrospect he could understand why it felt as though that was the right way to deal with things at the time, but over seventy years later he was beginning to wonder what else he could have done in those lost years.

"Tell me," Joggle asked, disturbing Gerald's thoughts. "How did you know I am an irk? We are exceptionally rare."

Gerald could tell from the emphasis Joggle placed on "exceptionally" that exceptional was the part of the sentence the irk really wanted him to focus on, although it was also true that they were very few in numbers. The question pulled Gerald back to the here and now, away from the dark memories that were slowly seeping back into his head.

"My mum," Gerald replied, a softness creeping into his voice that had not been there before. Joggle thought he saw a smile ignite in the man's eyes that wasn't quite able to make it to his lips before he continued speaking. "She would tell me stories of the old world, of the Guardians, and the birds and the beasts – of which I believe you are one."

8

Joggle's tail twitched and his face scrunched up as though he had just nibbled on a bad nut. "Beasts indeed. I'll have you know we are highly intelligent, highly knowledgeable, and highly articulate."

"I'm sorry," Gerald stuttered, caught on the back foot somewhat by the extent of Joggle's indignation. "I didn't mean to offend you."

It had been a long time since Gerald had last had a conversation with anyone other than himself. Despite his earlier trepidations about reaching out to the owner of the new voice, he was now glad that he had. Although clearly holding himself in high esteem, Joggle seemed generally good-natured, and Gerald had secretly yearned for company over the years.

"You said you were visiting. How long for?" Gerald asked.

"Not long. Never very long these days. Maybe another day or so? There is so much in the world to see, and it keeps on changing," Joggle said. "Especially since you humans started to flourish."

"Well, I would very much appreciate your company whilst you're here," Gerald replied earnestly.

"I would be happy to provide you with said company. If you like, I could regale you with tales of my expeditions, my journeys around the world and beyond the Void," Joggle said, thinking he could use the opportunity to find out more about the lad.

Gerald nodded. "That would be good. Maybe over breakfast?"

Joggle readily agreed, and as soon as Gerald had prepared a basic meal of bread and cheese, the pair sat by the lake and the irk began to talk. As Gerald had suspected talking was something the irk did well, particularly about subjects in which he considered himself to be an expert, which was apparently anything that he talked about. Breakfast soon turned into lunch, and lunch into dinner. For a second night Gerald did not sit waiting for sleep; instead, he sat listening intently to the little creature. It did not matter to him that he did not get more than two or three words in all day; he really did not have many stories to tell, and even fewer that he wanted to share. So, he listened attentively to everything the irk told him about the world he had spent most of his life hiding away from. Then, as the embers of the fire started to die, he asked Joggle when he would next return to the lake.

"In a few decades," Joggle answered without giving the matter much thought. "Of course, you'll be gone by then."

"Pardon? Do you know something I don't?" Gerald asked with a start. "Do you think old age might actually have caught me up by then?"

"I will not even pretend to know what your age will do. Although based on my previous visits, I would be very surprised if you looked any different from the way you do today, and weren't just as alive," Joggle said. Deep furrows suddenly lined Gerald's forehead and he looked confused. The irk continued, "Clearly this is not something your mother told you about. Sanctuary does not last forever, my friend, just a mere one hundred years."

"What happens then? Do I just get kicked out?" Gerald asked.

"Metaphorically so. My understanding is that the Guardians withdraw their protection from around the lake. Then anyone and everyone really will be able to find you, not just those of us well versed in the art of cross-dimensional navigation," Joggle explained.

Gerald sat quietly contemplating this new information. For the first time in his life, it dawned on him, he needed to really consider the future. It had never been a thing he had considered before, and what made it harder was that he had to consider that future outside the sanctuary - outside what had become not only his home, but also his entire world.

"You've gone quiet," Joggle pointed out unhelpfully.

"Are you sure about the hundred-year thing? Like you said, mum never mentioned it in any of her stories," Gerald asked, a nervous quiver detectable in his voice.

"Quite sure. Your mother clearly had an impressive understanding of the world, but few have the learnings of millennia I am able to draw upon," Joggle replied, with the same misplaced reassurance in his tone with which he had informed Gerald that there were most certainly paths into the sanctuary.

"Hmmm," came Gerald's non-committal reply, before he stood up and started to walk away.

"Hey, where are you going?" Joggle asked, scurrying down from the log, and bounding into the long grass by the path in his best attempt to keep up.

"I... I think I have... some thinking to do," Gerald faltered as he spoke. "If you don't mind, I think it's time I went to bed."

The final words were said with a surprisingly abrupt firmness and accompanied by the closing of the door to the little hut. Joggle felt the door was closed with the intention of a slam, but the door lacked the craftsmanship and heavy materials required to make it happen.

Joggle sat outside in the dark feeling a little dejected and unsure of what he had done, or said, to provoke this reaction. He had enjoyed the day, although somehow, despite talking to Gerald throughout almost the entirety of it, he had not managed to learn anything about the lad, other than his name and that he had a very knowledgeable mother. These things were not, in themselves, overwhelmingly useful pieces of information though. After a few seconds of waiting, just in case the lad reappeared, he shrugged his shoulders, his nose twitched, and a little while later he was back amongst the canopies, the day's final nut in hand. He would try to find out more tomorrow, he thought to himself.

Chapter 3

Joggle's revelation about the limited time he had remaining in the sanctuary had much the same result as a red-hot poker being applied to Gerald's bare behind. It created a hugely uncomfortable feeling he could not ignore and made sitting comfortably an impossibility. He paced nervously around the small hut, clenching and unclenching his fists. His poor command of numbers meant he had not understood that he still had twenty years left until the protections he now relied upon were withdrawn. Listening in awe to the little creature's stories of his adventures throughout the day had made Gerald too embarrassed to say anything that might make him seem, even more, like the cowardly idiot he had now convinced himself he was.

The embarrassment of not being able to work out how many years he still had hidden away from the world fuelled his anxieties, causing his mind to race between his many different fears and concerns, never settling on any long enough to properly think them through. He tried his best to focus on one thing at a time, but regardless of whether he thought about his past, his present, or his future, there was nothing that ignited even the smallest spark of excitement, or at the very least made him feel even slightly good about himself.

He eventually settled on the cherished memories of his mum, made more perfect by the passage of time. They had been poor, but he always remembered having a happy life with her. He wondered what advice she would give him now. But even as he did so, he felt tears in the corners of his eyes as he reminded himself that he would never know. She had undoubtedly passed away by now and he had been too scared and too selfish to ever visit her. Was it really the first time, he thought, that he'd realised he should have brought her back to the sanctuary with him so they could have been together? Maybe whatever had happened to him to halt his ageing might have happened to her as well, and she would still be with him.

This, he reminded himself as he used the end of his sleeve to blot a tear that had started to roll down his cheek, was why he never dwelt on the past. Because every time he did so he could not help but see his existence as a series of follies and mistakes that only seemed to hurt other people: follies that had cost people their homes, and mistakes that had cost them their lives. It was why he never thought about the future; because any future he might want, he felt he did not deserve, and the future he thought he deserved, he did not want. And so those precious, perfect memories of his mum quickly faded to flames, panic, fear, and death.

Stealing, he thought, that was at the root of it all. If he had not stolen the bread from the bakery, he would not have knocked over the little oil lamp that set the village alight. If he had not left the sanctuary to steal that flower, he was pretty sure he would not have woken up surrounded by the remains of all those poor people. And whilst he did not understand the connection between those bodies and his actions, he could not imagine a situation where they were not linked in some way.

He wondered what would have happened if he had simply not stolen the bread, but he knew it would have taken all these wasted years to convince him not to. There had been no money for food that week. There had been no money for anything at all after the rent had been paid, and so he stole.

He liked to think that he was a good thief - not in the sense that he was particularly skilled or accomplished, but that he only stole what they needed to survive, to supplement the meagre scraps his mum would optimistically call meals. He never stole from anyone he felt would miss what he took. This was not just an attempt to keep his conscience clear, but very much a matter of practicality. Whilst he was poor compared to most of the people who lived in the village, they were also poor. Just slightly less poor than him. Most were labourers and tradespeople ultimately employed by the two landowners whose forefathers had managed to grab fields around the village, largely through violence, decades before. He knew from his own experience that people with the fewest possessions tended to notice thefts the quickest, because the less you have the more likely you are to notice that things have gone missing, and so would be that little bit quicker to start looking for thieves.

Another way that Gerald used to salve his conscience was by believing that he was also a very bad thief. So bad that the whole village knew full well about his crimes, but for some reason, perhaps because they felt sorry for him and his mum, they were happy to turn a blind eye. This was not the case. From the very first time his mum had found an apple in her bag, that the six-year-old Gerald had taken from a small trader at the weekly market, his crimes had gone undetected. Though he did not realise it, because he had never had the cause or circumstance to compare himself to others, he was possessed of a predisposition for many talents required by the very best of thieves.

13

So, as he once again convinced himself that the fire was as inevitable as the theft which led to it, he started to remember the village that morning, before the sun had risen. Flames danced, smoke billowed, and people ran screaming from their ramshackle homes. It had happened during the summer; he remembered so clearly the shouts for water, but there was no water. At least not enough to quench the flames that spread so quickly between the dry thatched roofs. Panic had turned to helplessness, and the moment it became clear there was someone to blame, the helplessness had become anger, then judgement, and finally an unspoken agreement between the villagers that it was time for an execution. Torches lit from flaming homes had chased him from the village, across the fields, over the heathland, and up the hills towards the woods. He had run for almost fifteen miles with the mob at his heels, his youth providing just enough energy to keep him ahead of them until they reached that last steep, rock-strewn hill that led to the forest.

As he ran, he had recited the prayers of protection his mum had made him say every night before bed. Not because he thought they would work, but because he had nothing else to cling to, so he had clung to the only thing he had left. It came as quite a shock when the Guardians had answered him, whispered directions in his ears, guided his feet to the lake and, most impressively of all, moved the trees to create an impenetrable barrier, at least as he knew now, to those particular pursuers.

Thinking about it in the quiet of his hut brought all the emotions rushing back - the fear and the panic, all tinged with the thrill of staying one step ahead. Then came the exuberance of survival, the realisation that he had made it and was beyond their reach. And finally came the relief that it was all over, that the place he found himself in was so beautiful, so calming. He had laid down in the grass by the lake and fallen into a deep slumber, only to awake fully rested the next morning. And what an awakening that had been. He remembered the sound of bird song and the smell of flowers. He had been amazed by the beauteous riot of colour and movement, the sheer volume of life that seemed to share the sacred space. Everywhere he looked butterflies and bees flitted and buzzed, busy in their daily routines. But above everything he remembered the lake. It stretched out as far as the eye could see. The crystal-clear water afforded a view to the bottom, where fish swam. He washed in it, and it was warm. He drank from it, and it quenched his thirst. He smiled and swam all day, and then slept another night in the long grass beneath a blanket of stars. It was as if the world had been made new around him and he was the only person in it.

To begin with he had told himself his stay would be brief, just long enough for the furore of the fire to pass, and time enough for wounds to heal and anger to calm. He decided he would rest there, by the lake for a few days, and then slip back into the village to see his mum. He knew it was likely to be risky. He had a fair idea how the villagers would react if they discovered him, and he knew it was likely to involve a noose.

Unsurprisingly the idea terrified the lonely twelve-year-old boy. Then, without an education or grounding in numbers he soon lost track of time. Days turned into weeks, and weeks to seasons, and suddenly he was so much older. The terror felt by the twelve-year-old was replaced by the uncertainty isolation creates about the world outside. Fear kept him tethered to the grove and prevented him from leaving. Then he heard the voice, the first voice.

Gerald had another sleepless night, as he continued to think the thoughts he did his utmost to avoid on a daily basis. He started to realise that there was an irony to it all. He had always believed he had escaped - escaped the mob and then whatever had chased him from the brothel. But to what end? What had he achieved? He was still alive, but for all the time he had survived he had created nothing. In the time that he had spent throwing stones into the lake, more motivated people would have built a house, or a castle, an empire even. He had built nothing. He could not even take credit for the hut. The hut had been there when he arrived, with the bed, the chair, the table, and the small chest that was now filled with his meagre belongings. Nor could he take all the credit for feeding himself. The grove, or maybe some spirit or sprite, would leave packages of meat and cheese and bread for him around the lake so he did not need to hunt or bake, simply forage for fruit and vegetables to accompany his meals.

He had just about managed to make ill-fitting clothes from old bedding, but that had been out of necessity as he outgrew the clothes he had arrived in, and though they were comfortable and warm, they were not pretty and were definitely not for the world outside. Any thoughts he had to the contrary were swiftly dismissed by the first voice. That voice had provided him with fresh clothes for his journey. However, by the time he returned to the sanctuary they were torn and stained, and though he washed them in the lake and did his best to repair them, he could not bring himself to wear them again.

Eventually his thoughts returned him to the present, back with all the fear and self-loathing, but now things had changed. He could no longer live his life solely in the present, ignoring the past and the future. The future had finally tracked him down. It was coming for him, and his world was going to change whether he liked it or not. Maybe it was the fear of change, or maybe it was the irk's stories that suddenly inspired and emboldened him; whatever it was, he found himself lifting the lid of the small wooden chest again. He unpacked the clothes he had not worn for around seventy years and laid them out on the bed. He opened a small purse of coins, took some out and looked at them, wondering if they still had any value. He knew there was only one way he would find out.

Once everything he needed had been removed from the box, one item remained, a small white shirt. It was stained with grass and mud and soot. He buried his face in it and found the smell of smoke still lingered, even after all those years. He felt his tears rise again, but this time he made no effort to hold them back.

Chapter 4

Gerald walked with a sense of purpose for the first time in decades. There were many miles to be covered, fifteen in all. It had been so long since he had last journeyed anywhere outside the forest, but his feet still remembered the old path. It was the path he had walked so many times with his mum: first as a toddler, holding her hand as he stumbled over pebbles and uneven ground, then as a child fighting grass dragons with sticks. Finally, as an almost teenager fleeing a mob, half of whom would have happily seen him hanged in the market square - if they could keep him alive long enough to get him back to the village after the other half had got their hands on him.

For the first ten miles or so, the going was easy. It was a good day for travelling. The weather was warm, and the sun was behind him. The ground didn't feel as though it had changed much underfoot. It was still uneven, still littered with rocks hidden from the eye by long grasses and ferns, and most importantly still downhill.

The morning seemed to fly by. He felt carefree, just as he had all those years ago holding his mum's hand, and for the first time in a long time he felt strangely unburdened. He pushed aside the heavy, clouding thoughts of the past few days. The sun warmed him, and a breeze set the long grass waving around him. It reminded him of younger, happier times when he had all the world before him, but didn't know it, and had no concerns about anything outside of the bubble that contained his mum and his village.

Slowly the slope evened, and the grass got shorter. Rocks either seemed fewer and further between, or easier to spot, allowing him to increase his pace. Inevitably the first signs of people came. A herd of sheep grazed on what was now short scrappy grassland. It was not so much the sheep themselves that jolted Gerald out of his pleasant daydreams, but the dark blue crosses dyed into their fleeces. It was an unwelcome reminder that he was about to face the people whose homes he had destroyed, and even though he knew it had happened a long time ago, he could not help but worry about how they might react to his return.

The sheep meant the village was close now. His stomach suggested it was sometime after lunch, although this was a far from reliable measure of the hour. All the same, he continued on his way. Soon sheep were replaced by cows, kept closer to the village because of the daily need for milk, and finally houses appeared in the distance. He stopped and took in the view. It wasn't anything like he remembered; even at this distance he could see the village had grown into a town that covered at least three times the land the village once had. He continued walking and soon discovered a wide dirt road he had no memory of heading towards the town, wide enough that a wagon and rider could travel side by side along it. Every so often he would see stones with letters or numbers of some sort carved into them, which he assumed were signs for Spindle, or what had once been Spindle, what had once been his home.

He paused by one to catch his breath and pondered its implications. There had never been signs in, let alone to, Spindle when he was younger. Not only was the village too small and insignificant for anyone to really need to go there, but as the majority of the population could neither read nor write there was no value in having them, and even less value in the effort that would have been expended in making them. Now, though, the signs only served to provide more evidence to support the recurring suspicion Gerald had that, a better person than he would have used their time in the sanctuary far more constructively.

Looking further down the road to where the village – now a town he reminded himself – nestled, it was clear that, whilst he had been wasting his days throwing stones into a lake, the villagers had rebuilt their homes and carried on with their lives. Unknown to Gerald, in addition to the new homes, roads and signs, there had also been a series of name changes. A rapid succession of new names that had peaked in verbosity with Spindle-new-town-built-upon-the-remains-of-old-Spindle-village, before the technically more concise, but almost as unwieldy, Spindle-Upon-Spindle had finally been settled on by the town assembly.

He reached the outermost dwellings of the town and found that they were just as he remembered, small and makeshift in appearance. But these types of buildings had once made up the village in its entirety: ramshackle homes that just about stood up to the elements, homes of necessity. Because it was necessary to have somewhere dry and out of the wind to spend time between the long days in the fields. Comfort was never a priority for people who lived in houses like these, just as he had; it was a luxury, and luxuries were something there was never the time or money for.

He passed by the necessary dwellings and soon found himself surrounded by what felt like hundreds of larger timber-framed buildings. These had much more of a look of permanence about them with their thick,

18

externally visible support beams painted in blacks and greys, and their clay-tiled roofs. The people of the town were clearly, in the main, doing well for themselves. He saw this reflected not only in the size and quality of the new homes, but also in the colour that punctuated the city streets. With each step it became apparent that the homeowners had developed a penchant for painting the plaster panels that filled the spaces between the beams with bright colours. In truth hundreds of houses was something of an exaggeration, but he did not have the words at his disposal to describe the thriving town his poor village had become.

Now there were more homes, and presumably more people, he wondered if a proper market square had been established. The market square of Spindle had been nothing more than a scrap of unworkable land within shouting distance of the houses. There wasn't a regular market day that attracted traders from outside the village, but occasionally a travelling trader would stumble across Spindle and pitch up for the night. They would normally offer their goods for a few hours on the off chance of attracting some business, before moving on to their intended destination early the next morning.

Gerald continued to follow the road without noticing that, at some point, the dirt track he had started walking on had become a cobbled street, so intrigued was he by the changes that had occurred whilst he had been away. He moved instinctively towards the centre of the town, drawn along by the noise, the sights, and the smells of this new world. Suddenly the cobbled street turned a corner, and Gerald found himself in the market square.

It was busy. He was surprised at just how many people were moving around the little stalls and hand carts that advertised their wares with shouts, placards, bells, and apparently even the odd blast of a horn. As well as the traders with their makeshift storefronts, there was a number of small shops, including herbalists, hairdressers, bakers and butchers, that had established themselves in the buildings that surrounded and defined the square. With the exception of an inn, all had their goods, services or tools on display. They seemed to be as popular as the little market stalls, with townsfolk bustling in and out of them.

Gerald felt a little overwhelmed by all the people, but then he had never been one for large groups. He had visited one of the biggest cities on the continent, Tanglehaven, just once in his whole life and had been left speechless by the experience. He had been quite taken aback by the sheer amount of life crammed into one place. The heave and pitch of so many people thrown together, out of what he thought was their own choice, had left him feeling claustrophobic and eager to escape. Strangely though, it had also made him feel isolated, anonymous, and as disconnected as he felt in the forest.

The huge number of people and stretched resources of the city created a different kind of necessity to the kind he had experienced growing up. The necessity of the villagers was that of the time poor. In the countryside there were the resources to create and build the things you needed, so finding the time to do it was the challenge.

In the city, not only were people time poor, just as they were in the countryside, but resources seemed to be spread thin. In the village if you wanted a chair but could not afford to buy one, you found wood, brought it home and fashioned one. But in the city, there was no wood lying around waiting to be found, and so necessity became desperation. And desperation was what he had found around every corner where the normal people lived, the people like him and his mum. Yes, there were areas of the city where desperation did not seem to be, like the big house he had stolen the flower from. But even those houses with their high walls topped with spikes, and the guards in the streets outside, hinted at their own particular type of desperation - to protect what they had and keep those who might try to take it from them out. He knew almost as soon as he arrived it was not a world he wanted to be a part of.

By contrast the town seemed to be at a happy mid-point where people had more than was necessary, and desperation was not yet obvious on every street corner. Although he had no doubt that behind the doors to the most ramshackle homes, desperation was already creeping through the cracks. Just as he was sure that the homes of the town's richest inhabitants would be found behind the same high walls with their spikes. The town's growth surprised him; it was a world away from what he had expected to find. In his mind the village had never grown, or even changed. He felt foolish admitting to himself that he would have been less surprised if he had been met by the same ragged little buildings, housing the same people who had chased him all those years ago. Joggle was right, humans did have a habit of thriving and flourishing, given enough time. Did that make him an exception?

For the first time, Gerald really became aware of the people milling around him as people, rather than a backdrop. He started to notice them looking at him. Not everyone, but there was the occasional sideways glance, or a pointing child, who was quickly admonished by their parent for noticing someone who looked a bit different in such a way that almost always makes the original transgression so much more obvious. He breathed a sigh of relief that whatever was drawing people's attention did not seem to be a general recognition that he had, albeit many years ago, burnt the place to the ground.

At first, he thought it might simply be because he was a stranger, unknown in the town. But then he reasoned that there was no way anyone could know everyone in a town this size. It was only as he made his way around the market stalls, in search of some food, that the source of his interest to people became apparent. A barber called out to him from his shop, asking him if he would like a haircut and beard trim. Realisation dawned. Such had been his rush to leave that morning, and his interest in the new world he found himself in, he had completely forgotten that several decades of hair and beard growth had accumulated since he had last been anywhere with a mirror, let alone with the facilities to address the situation. Gerald laughed and waved the man away at first, saying that he doubted he could afford his services. The man continued to pester him, and Gerald was, in truth, quite keen on the idea of parting with his shaggy locks. So, after a little prevarication he approached the man and offered him a coin for his services. The man was taken aback.

"You are indeed a very modest man to believe you could not afford my services, sir," the hairdresser said politely, ushering Gerald to his chair, before sharpening his blades enthusiastically.

Gerald sat and watched as the man set about the not inconsiderable task of taming his hair. He could not help but think of Joggle as the hairdresser proceeded to cut and talk, asking questions he wanted no answers to, as they only served as a bridge between topics the barber wished to speak about. Gerald found the constant babble oddly relaxing and let the man's words flow around him, paying only enough attention to ensure he contributed the odd grunt of agreement whenever there was a silence long enough to allow one in. Once relieved of the majority of his hair, he paid with the coin he had fished out of his pouch, and the hairdresser provided him with a handful of smaller coins in return. Gerald looked at him in surprise.

"Change," the man said by way of explanation. Having never really had anything to do with money, it was not a concept Gerald understood, but he took it at face value and pocketed the loose coins.

"A quick question, my friend," Gerald said to the hairdresser, his stomach excited that his small collection of coins seemed to have value. "Where would be the closest place to eat?"

"The Muddy Toad, sir," the man replied, pointing to the inn on the other side of the square. "Not the most salubrious of establishments, but it serves a good pie and a very nice pint of ale. Very popular with the traders."

"Thank you," Gerald replied, his stomach already urging him towards the door as quickly as it thought his legs would be able to convey him across the square. Looking less like a mobile hedge, Gerald noticed that the glances were now fewer and there were no more shussing sounds from embarrassed parents. Of the glances that still did come his way, though, he noticed almost all could be considered admiring.

He walked through the door of the Muddy Toad and the smell of hot food rushed to meet him, just about beating the smell of ale-dampened floorboards and pipe tobacco. He was not sure whether it was the excitement of discovering the new town that had grown up on the site of the old village, or the relief that decrepit villagers kept from their graves by their desire to lynch him had not been his welcoming party, that had suppressed the hunger he had felt coming into the town, but now it was back with a vengeance.

He strode up to the bar, made his requests and several minutes later tucked into a large meat pie and generous pint of ale. He felt content, but somewhat at a loose end. He had to be honest that this wasn't how he expected the day to go. It was obviously a better outcome than dangling from the end of a rope, but all the same he realised that he had no further business in the town, in part because the town was no longer his village. It had become something else, something that he no longer felt any connection to. It was an odd feeling, so faced with the choice of a fifteen-mile walk back to the sanctuary, which he now considered his home, or another pint, he opted for the latter.

This quickly turned into a third pint, and as alcohol and loneliness generally increase the attractiveness of one whilst ensuring a continuation of the other, a fourth pint soon made its way from the bar to his table. As a non-drinker the alcohol quickly went to his head, so when the fourth pint arrived, things were already starting to go downhill. By the time it was finished the bottom of the hill had been reached and he had been sick all over it. Despite that, and seemingly at the behest of a small crowd that had materialised around him, a fifth pint appeared, and he continued to drink until he passed out.

Chapter 5

The awakening could have been described as gentle. Chag, the Muddy Toad's cleaner, bar worker and doorman certainly considered it to be so. When he had arrived for work, Darl, the innkeeper, had asked the moleman to clean around the stranger, but to not be afraid to give him the odd nudge. She wanted the stranger to be functional by the time the cleaning was done, and the inn ready to open again. Chag obliged. Whilst this kind of thing was infrequent, it was not unknown that Darl would occasionally let the truly hammered sleep it off on the bar's tables and benches. Of course, there would be an extra penny added to the bill for bed and board, and an extra penny for the additional clean-up Chag would have to do, which Darl would always put straight into his pocket. There was also the very high expectation of a suitably large gratuity suggested politely by Darl, with the supporting politeness of the broad-shouldered moleman and his clean and exceedingly well-kempt claws, that would immediately be split between the two of them.

"Wha'aaa," were Gerald's very first words, followed a few seconds later by "Ungh" and "Ga bur?".

The moleman ignored the grunts and continued to mop the floor, letting the end of the mop handle occasionally jab into Gerald's ribs when angles and proximity allowed. Chag had also positioned his dirty water bucket just behind Gerald's chair. So once consciousness had been grasped, the repugnant aromas, in addition to the jabs, quickly moved Gerald from grunts to words, and from blinking to sight.

"Do you have to do that?" Gerald asked as the frequency of the jabs seemed to increase, or maybe it was his capacity to feel them that was improving.

"Do you have to be here?" Chag snapped back, without looking up, in a gruff voice.

"Well…" Gerald started to say, before remembering that at that precise moment there was nowhere else for him to be, and that he wasn't entirely sure where the "here" in Chag's question actually was.

When the bar was cleaned and the jabbing had stopped, Chag disappeared into the kitchen and Gerald sat alone in the welcome silence, his head pounding. He watched light streaming through clusters of small windows around the door, wondering what to do next, but nothing sprang

24

to mind. So, in lieu of a more pressing activity, he stared blankly as the dust particles the light illuminated flitted about in the air, readying themselves to undo the good work of the moleman.

Darl walked down the stairs from her lodgings above. Gerald turned at the sound of her feet descending, although not as sharply as he would have under less hungover circumstances.

"How are you feeling this morning my little fire-starter?" Darl asked. She had a strong accent that Gerald wasn't familiar with, but it forced the common words of the local tongue into a near musical experience that the native speakers certainly weren't able to achieve, and Gerald found himself instantly warming to her. Her broad smile and friendly face made him feel welcome, although he noted a hardness in her green eyes, which he assumed came from dealing with people who did not handle their drinks well. She had long auburn hair that was drawn up and tied back. She wore a white blouse, buttoned to the neck, and a long burgundy skirt that stopped an inch or so above simple brown shoes.

Seconds later, his brain caught up with what she had said, and the little composure he had recovered shattered.

"What's that meant to mean?" he attempted to ask, although a combination of shock, tiredness and bemusement meant the question was barely audible.

Darl had been running bars for long enough to know that the first words of the passed out returning to the land of the sober and awake are seldom, "Good morning. How are you?" or "Thank you for your kind hospitality". Normally these sorts of conversation starters are replaced with questions that serve to help the waking understand where they are, or what the holy hell had happened to them the night before, or why a moleman was jabbing them with a mop handle.

"Memory loss?" she asked.

"Apparently so," Gerald said, now fully alert. Despite the pounding headache, and the certainty that he would be unlikely to make it off the bench without throwing up again, adrenalin was flowing, and instinct was taking over. Suddenly he found himself watching Darl very carefully. "Why did you call me a fire-starter?" he asked, in a voice that had just about made it to the verge of being suitable for talking.

He noticed Darl's body language change. Although she still sounded carefree and cheery, she seemed to be making a point of keeping a distance from him. Whereas before she had been heading directly towards him, she had suddenly found a distraction that had taken her back to the bar, several metres from where he sat.

Gerald's response to her greeting had spooked her. He was clearly defensive about the manner in which she had addressed him, and that was not what she had been hoping for. Alcohol loosens tongues, and some tongues end up a bit too loose, occasionally spilling words the tongue's owner will regret the next morning. More often than not though, what comes out of the mouths of drunks is little more than harmless lies and exaggerations, intended to make the speaker seem so much more than they are in reality. Generally, those outbursts are embarrassing more than revealing, but in Gerald's case what he had said fell categorically into the revealing bucket. Darl had initially ignored the drunken young man and his claims that he had been responsible for burning the village down. But that all changed when he started to talk about the rose he had stolen. Darl had thought carefully that night about how to broach the subject with him the next morning, and whether it was even a good idea. She decided that rather than jump straight in with a flurry of questions about his misadventures in Tanglehaven, she would tease him about the fire the twenty-something-looking man had started eighty odd years ago. She hoped that in the cold light of day he would admit to claiming the actions of others as his own, before sloping off in embarrassment, hopefully never to be seen again.

"Don't worry, you didn't burn anything down," she said. "You just told a few tall tales about setting the old village alight."

She paused to see how Gerald would react. Panic filled his face.

"Of course," she said, noting his reaction. "Most people in here aren't old enough to remember the old village, let alone the fire. And let's face it, you're clearly not old enough to have had anything to do with it. A couple of the older regulars thought it was in bad taste though."

The panic plastered over Gerald's face eased slightly.

"But it's not like they have any reason to be upset. The way I understand it none of them grew up in the old village anyway," she said, watching Gerald relax and treating him to another of her broad smiles. "That's the thing about humans though - always looking for something to get excited about. I mean, if I had a penny for each time one of them told me that their parents thought the old village was at its best immediately after it had been burnt down... well, I certainly wouldn't need to be running this place anymore. The old boys just like something to complain about."

She laughed and watched as Gerald forced out a nervous chuckle.

"Yeah," he said. "Old people certainly like a good moan."

"You fancy a drink and something to eat before you head off?" she asked.

Gerald's stomach lurched into his throat at the mere mention of eating. "Erm, no food thanks, but some water would be welcome," he replied.

Deciding he presented no immediate danger, she poured him a mug of tepid well water from a jug on the bar. She carried it to him and sat down on the other side of the table. He reached for it, and thirstily put it to his lips.

Darl understood people and knew how to set them at ease. It was her talent, her power. It was the reason she had ended up running inns and why, over her many years, she had built so many successful businesses. It was easy when you knew exactly what your customers wanted better than they did. Now awake, Gerald was easy to read, but despite that there was something about him that just didn't seem to add up. He was, in appearance at least, human. Yet if his stories were truly his, he would now be far beyond the age at which most humans passed on to the world beyond. But Darl knew only too well how little appearances should be relied upon.

"You know," she said, carefully trying to keep her tone conversational even though what she was about to say was intended to test Gerald further. "One of the things I love about my job is hearing local legends. There are some folks who think the fire is the most interesting thing about this place, but I think it's the story about the mother of the boy who started it."

Gerald paused between gulps but didn't look up from his mug. Darl continued, "It's not a very long story, but very tragic. Apparently, after the villagers chased him away, she waited at the edge of the village for him to return, refusing to eat, drink or sleep in case she missed him if he ever came back to visit. She was worried that if he came back the villagers might arrest him and hang him before she could give him, at the very least, a final hug goodbye. But the lad never returned. So, in the end she just faded away. It's such a sad story, don't you think?"

The reaction was immediate and involuntary. Gerald felt tears well up in his eyes. He swallowed hard, trying his best to contain his emotions, whilst keeping the mug firmly in front of his face in the hope that Darl would not see.

She continued, "The townsfolk say she's buried on top of the small hill in the temple grounds, under the old oak tree. The Guardian, the villagers used to call it. Apparently, they all felt so bad about chasing her son away, they thought the least they could do was lay her to rest in a place with a good view of the surrounding countryside. That way she could continue her watch for his return."

As Darl spoke about where his mum had been laid to rest, Gerald noticed a slight change in her tone. It was subtle, and he couldn't quite put his finger on what it was, but there was something about what she had said, or the way she had said it, that he felt should have troubled him. However, he had no capacity or desire in that moment to dig through, or even challenge, the woman's words. The heady combination of the hangover and the emotional response to her story meant there was now only one thing on his mind. But before he sought to address it, one final question demanded an answer.

"Are there any stories about what happened to the boy? You know, after he ran away?" Gerald asked, voice wobbling as he tried to contain his emotions.

"A few. Almost all say he survived. Most of the stories I've heard say that he simply outran the mob, but there are a couple of more fanciful tales out there. There is one old man in the town who claims his dad was leading the chase. He says his dad saw the trees themselves surround the boy, hiding him from the villagers and stopping them from getting at him," she said, her voice back to its cheerful flow. "I'm not sure how much I believe it though; sounds more like someone trying to save face if you ask me. Anyway, I'm sure I don't need to tell you that people do tell the most fanciful stories. Especially in tiny villages filled with superstitious farm workers. Don't worry, no one took you seriously last night. Let's face it, if you'd really had anything to do with it, you'd be about a hundred by now, and look like a walking corpse!"

"Which, of course, you don't," she added with a smile and a wink.

With the subject of conversation switching away from his mum, Gerald managed to get a grip on his emotions. He lowered the mug, smiled, and even managed a bit of a forced chuckle at Darl's final remarks, although the wink caught him off guard. Darl noted Gerald's relief, she assumed, at her apparent disbelief that he could have had anything to do with the fire, and the conversation came to an end.

Darl stood, made her excuses, and returned to the bar. She was interested to see what the lad would do next. In the brief time they spoke that morning she developed an instinctive fondness for him. He looked young, but based on the stories he had told, which she now believed to be true, he had to be at least ninety. Yet there was a disarming naivety about

28

him, which she would never have associated with the sort of master thief that, she assumed, would be needed to steal the rose.

After a few more minutes of sitting in silence Gerald decided it was time to leave. He wanted to find out if the woman was telling the truth about his mum. He walked to the bar, paid, and thanked the woman for letting him stay. It was only after he left, he realised that he had not introduced himself, at least not that he remembered. He shrugged, as he felt it unlikely that he would ever see her again, before continuing on his way.

He left the inn sometime around eleven o'clock that morning. The fresh air brought his appetite back. He stopped at one of the bakers in the market square for a loaf of bread, which he nibbled on as he set out for the temple. He asked for directions as he went, and as he approached the building it was apparent that it too had benefited from the new-found wealth in the town. Although the building was still there, its weather-worn stonework standing out in a town of relatively new, dark timber-framed buildings with their colourful plaster walls, the old temple had grown. It had brand new stone extensions branching out from either side of the original building, presumably to make space for the growing faithful of the growing town.

Whenever he thought about the village, the ramshackle buildings it had consisted of always faded into a general remembrance of closely packed thatched roofs and tiny windows. The temple, however, had remained firmly fixed in his memory because it had been made of stone, with a slate roof. As a youngster he had always wondered why a village of people so busy with surviving would expend their precious time constructing a building more watertight, and secure, than their own homes. Especially since they would then go on to spend as little time as possible in it, and actively invent reasons to not have to go to it.

The people of Spindle, as with so many things, had taken a highly pragmatic approach to religion. Rather than wasting their time arguing about whether there was a god, or some gods, or whether the temple should be in honour of a particular god, they had simply built a temple, just in case. Although no one had managed to satisfactorily explain just in case of what. There had been one of those general agreements that a temple was something villages had. So, since no one in the village had ever met a god, and not a single member of the community felt that Spindle would ever be of any real interest to a god, there seemed no reason to do very much more than that.

When someone did eventually raise a question as to whether their approach was just a bit short-sighted and try to explain that this was not what religion was all about, they were labelled a zealot and invested as the village priest. The new priest was then told, in no uncertain terms, that the whole religion thing was their problem to deal with. And, whilst they had free rein to do whatever they thought was right, it should in no way interfere with the general day-to-day lives of the villagers, and not be too expensive. There had been a small group of regular worshippers, Gerald remembered, but only because he and his mum had been two of them. Even with the temple, religion had remained something of a fringe interest in Spindle.

Whilst Gerald still lived in the village, the temple had been set apart from the main clump of buildings. Now, with the growth of the town there were unbroken streets of houses leading up to it, and a row of five large, detached houses with walls around them topped with tall metal spikes standing opposite. He noticed, looking between gaps in the homes that lined the street leading to the temple, that the graveyard still lay behind the building. The cynic in him suddenly started to wonder if the extension work on the temple had actually happened at about the same time as the houses with the high walls had been built. Views, after all, were important.

By the time he came to a stop in front of the temple doors, he felt more like his usual self. The nibbles on his bread had turned to bites. His stomach had settled, and the fresh air had helped to order his thoughts. Swallowing down the last bite of bread he made his way towards the little hill, where the woman had said he would find his mother's grave.

The graveyard, like everything else, had grown over the years. It spread out as far as the eye could see and was, probably, one of the only parts of the original settlement that still met the countryside. Despite the growth, Gerald's mother's grave was instantly recognisable, just as the woman had said. There was a slight rise several metres from the rear of the temple where a large oak tree grew, and a single headstone sat in its shade. The Guardian still stands, Gerald thought to himself as he eyed the mighty oak. That had to be a good sign.

The walk to the headstone seemed longer than the walk from the sanctuary to the town. He felt a strange buzz of excitement, an elation that he could not rationalise with the reality of the situation. Gerald had been twelve when he had been chased from the village, and whilst in the eyes of some that had almost made him a man, he was still, in so many ways, a child. It was that child that he could feel inside him now, running towards the mother he hadn't seen for so many years, whilst the man struggled to hold him back. The man tried to calm the child and prepare him for the cold reality that the mother he had yearned to see for so long, the mother whose hugs he had longed for throughout the lonely nights in the forest, was no more - no more than a rock and a memory.

With each step the man and the boy vied for control, until they reached the rock and the reality overwhelmed them both in a rush of regret and a flood of tears. He doubled over and sank to his knees. He did not even try to stop the sadness that he had battled so desperately to hide behind the mug in the inn earlier that morning. Inside him the man and the boy asked the same questions knowing the answers were equal measures of fear, selfishness, survival, and stupidity. They always had been, but out of sight had kept them out of mind. Here, by her gravestone, they were now thrust into the light. They could no longer be ignored, and tear-choked fragments of "Sorry" and "I miss you, mumma" were the only words he could find to convey the whole mess of emotions that overcame him.

Darl watched from a safe distance. Seeing the stranger collapsed on the hill confirmed her worst fears. She reasoned that if one drunken, implausible story were true, it was highly likely that the other one was as well. Sometimes, although not often, she really hated being right.

It was mid-afternoon now, and the sun was high in the sky. Although it wasn't the burning heat of the Lost Lands, that Darl had found so unbearable, she stood in the shade of the temple. There was a reason why she liked her inn to be a bit gloomy, as some called it. The low light took the edge off people's senses, which meant they were less likely to notice the little details, the little tells and inconsistencies that got people wondering and whispering. These weren't bad things in themselves, as most people were generally accepting of others. However, occasionally those whispers found their way into the ears of the people who weren't as accepting and who worried about the others, the not-them. Sometimes those people worried so much they would get together and think of ways to resolve their worries, and those ways were never nice ways. So, Darl clung to the shadows, not just for protection against the heat, but for protection from those that might worry about her inconsistencies.

Minutes became hours and Gerald remained curled up on the rise. Darl began to wonder if he would ever leave. She wondered if he might end up as some did in the old stories, stories of loved ones who grieved so earnestly and so completely for their departed that they eventually became a part of the land they grieved upon. If she left now and returned tomorrow, would there be another hill in the graveyard, and would that be the end of his story? In some ways, Darl reflected, that might be the best end for him. But she suspected that this would not be the case, not because things like that didn't happen - they did - but because the young man had become part of another story. A much older story that had already travelled the world. And whilst his future was his own, as much as any of our futures are truly our own, he would not be able to avoid living in the shadow of the rose. He could choose to stay on that hill, reunited with his mother, but the shadow would continue to be cast.

More than all that, though, Darl was not about to let him get off the hook that easily. He did not know it, but she had been in the earliest stories of the rose that he had stolen, or the flower as he referred to it, oblivious to its bloody history. She had survived when others of her kind had not. When the rose, together with the stories about it, had finally vanished from people's memories she had breathed a sigh of relief, even though she knew the best stories are never lost for very long.

Gerald felt the hand on his shoulder long before he reacted to it. The boy closed his eyes and wished that it could be his mumma's hand. The man wished that the boy would not be disappointed, all the while knowing that was inevitable. Eventually he raised his tear-stained face for a few seconds before returning it, almost immediately, to the darkness of his palms as the boy tried to come to terms with the disappointment. Darl removed her hand and walked away. The touch was enough. He knew she was there. She moved closer to the Guardian, finding a comfortable patch of grass to sit on within its shade, taking care not to touch the silent giant.

Another half an hour passed, and Gerald was quiet, although he held his position and made no attempt to reach out to his audience. Darl started to feel restless. She hadn't known quite what to expect, but there was nothing that could have prepared her for the outpouring of emotion she was witnessing. Once again, she found herself questioning how, in the name of the heavens, this lad could have got caught up in all this mess. Regardless of the years he had accrued, he just seemed so young. She wanted to let him grieve, she wished she didn't have to be there intruding on such a private and personal moment, but she did. She needed to keep him close for now. She stood up and walked over to him. Scooping her skirts to one side, she squatted down so she could talk to him on the same level.

"Sorry to intrude, but I figured you might want someone here with you," she said, her accent a caressing softness in Gerald's ear.

Just as with so many things that had happened in the past few hours, Gerald felt confused. He wanted to be alone, he knew he wanted to be alone, but a sudden need for company seemed to be forcing itself on him. He couldn't tell when it had started, but he couldn't help but think it had been when she had arrived, or maybe it had been when she spoke. He found himself feeling as though he should want to be in her presence, even though he knew he just wanted to be left alone with his mum.

He suddenly felt angry at the stranger who had invaded his grief. He wanted to look her in the eye and tell her to leave him the hell alone, but something in her voice, maybe, stopped him from acting on the feelings he knew he felt. It was as though there was a net around him, that tightened every time he was about to say something. He looked up at her once again, a twitching in his eyes was the only thing he could do to convey the increasingly painful turmoil in his mind.

"I'm sorry, I happened to be passing and saw you." Darl lied lazily.

She paused for a few seconds, deciding what to do next, before continuing, "If you want a bed for the night, just pop by when you feel comfortable. I have a small spare room upstairs and it's yours for the night if you want it. Just ask for me at the bar. I'm Darl, by the way."

He nodded, and with that she gave him a brief hug before standing and bustling away.

Gerald heaved a sigh of relief that the woman had gone. The net that he had felt pressing in on him vanished. His mind was now clear and the feeling of being restrained had gone, but so had any clear memory of the conversation, or even the encounter. By the time he left the graveyard in the early evening he remembered only that Darl had offered him a place to stay at the Muddy Toad, which he reasoned must have happened over breakfast, because that was when he'd last seen her... wasn't it?

Darl hurried home from the temple through the busy streets. She never ran anywhere, but she had a way of moving with purpose when needed that got her places quickly. There was a steady pace, a determined look, and most helpfully a general feeling in those people either in her way, or likely to end up in her way, that this was the wrong place to be, and they really needed to do something about it. The resulting lack of impediment in the busy town streets lent her a significant advantage when trying to get around in a hurry.

For those crossing her path, or on course to do so, the feeling they responded to was not some tsunami of energy throwing people out of her way. It was not some aura of unimaginable terror projecting teeth and claws to shred their minds. It was not even really that noticeable. It was subtle, like a gentle whisper in your ear to turn slightly to the right before placing your next step. It was the unexpected need to stop walking momentarily because something you had never really been interested in had caught your eye, and you felt the need to confirm your continuing lack of interest in it with a quick glance. The feeling would make even the hardest and most ruthless of footpads and muggers pause to think of their mothers, or sisters, as Darl breezed by and out of immediate danger. The feeling lasted just the few seconds that Darl was in close proximity to her fellow pedestrians, and then disappeared with the sound of her footsteps. Unfortunately, in the case of the footpads and muggers the thoughts of mothers and sisters were also rapidly forgotten, and they immediately returned to their search for their next victims.

By the time she returned to the inn, the evening's busy period was getting underway. She glided through the closely packed huddles of customers, ignoring Chag's request for a hand behind the bar. Like Gerald and the citizenry of Spindle-Upon-Spindle, Chag was not immune to Darl's charms, and she never shied away from employing them when the occasion required. As she disappeared upstairs, Chag surveyed the customers and found himself deciding that he would be able to manage, at least for a little while longer, and started to pull the next pint. By the time the pint was on the bar, waiting to be picked up by a thirsty customer, Chag found himself wondering when Darl would return from her afternoon walk. It was not like her to be late for a shift, he thought, and it was starting to get busy.

Once upstairs, Darl, conscious that Chag was in fact rushed off his feet, quickly took some clean bedsheets from a small cupboard and prepared the single bed in the small spare room for Gerald. She didn't know for sure that he would return to the inn later, but she wanted to be ready in case he did. She wanted him to feel comfortable, and above all she wanted him to trust her. Partially, this was because she wanted him to open up about his time in Tanglehaven and the theft of the rose, but also because the fondness she had felt for him when they had spoken earlier that morning had deepened as she watched him at his mother's graveside. His grief had been so raw she could not believe him to be anyone but the small boy that had been chased from his mother's arms, and isolated from the world when he needed her the most. Despite the degree to which she had warmed to Gerald, she was under no illusions that there were still so many questions to be answered before she could trust him, and so she also wanted to keep at least one eye on him for the time being.

As she made up the bed for him, she couldn't help but wonder how he had got involved with the rose. She had heard snatches of his story the night before, but listening had been made difficult by the number of people who had gathered around him and his near-constant slurring. She wanted to hear everything.

She liked to see the good in people, it came naturally to her. However, a millennium of living alongside immortals and mortals had taught her the hard way that appearances could be deceiving. Some people were utterly evil, wicked to their cores, and yet it was not uncommon for those sorts of people to hide their poisonous thoughts and corrosive ambitions behind respectable veneers. From the moment Gerald had started speaking she had thought he was hiding something. The story about the fire had been inconsequential to her, but when he started to talk about the rose, she couldn't help but think the whole situation was too much of a coincidence. Of all the inns in all the world he could have gone into, why had it been hers? Someone whose world had already fallen under the flower's bloody shadow.

After he had passed out, Chag and Darl had spent the night watching him, knives in hands in case it had been an act. She had to admit to being a little surprised when it became apparent that he had actually drunk himself into oblivion and fallen asleep on the table in a pool of his own vomit. After that, she had thought about other ways she could test him. She almost felt guilty for making up the story about his mother and lying about the whereabouts of her grave, because the outpouring of grief had been so very real. The visit to the graveyard had also confirmed that he was unable to read, as the gravestone he had spent his afternoon in front of had been clearly inscribed with the name Robyrt Gurdge, which she had only discovered upon her arrival that afternoon. All in all, she thought to herself, if he was acting he was doing a damn good job, and he probably deserved to get away with whatever it was he was up to.

"Hey ho," she sighed as she finished by laying a folded blanket at the foot of the bed. "Being an immortal doesn't always mean you get to live forever."

A shout from downstairs snapped Darl back into the present. She remembered Chag was all on his own at what was peak time for a weekday. Darl's calming nature, or more accurately her nature of creating calm, whether it was wanted or not, meant her clientele could be a little unpredictable in her absence.

It's said a shady bar tends to attract shady customers, and this was certainly the case of the Muddy Toad. However, whilst Darl was keen on keeping the lights low, she was not keen on what would traditionally be considered shady behaviour, or any of the other attributes of bars that generally fell into the shady classification. As a result, those who ventured through the dark wooden door were met with a spotlessly clean venue (at opening time), comfortable furniture, reasonable food and, above all, decorum. The decorum was largely due to Darl's presence, but in her absence Chag's broad shoulders and sharp claws created a sort of fragile peace that generally held, provided the less reputable clientele had their needs met and didn't get sufficiently drunk to think annoying the moleman, or each other, was a good idea. Occasionally, the critical mass of Darl's absence, queues at the bar and Dutch courage was reached. Threats would be shouted, knives would come out and the odd chair would be broken, but it never lasted long once Chag got involved. The offenders soon found themselves bloody, beaten and lying in the gutter outside, deciding whether to run for it or wait for the Watch to scrape them off the pavement and provide them with accommodation for the night. As a result, the Muddy Toad had something of a mixed reputation within the town which just about lurched towards good.

On this particular evening the critical mass had been reached. Darl's unusually long absence from the bar, combined with a birthday celebration for one of the regulars, and a group of thirsty traders who were all trying to order drinks at the same time had created something of an incendiary situation. The regulars were drunk, but not so drunk that they were going to upset the moleman who was clearly working as fast as he could. Despite occasional fallings out, or possibly because of them, the regulars in question had a great respect for the old mercenary. Ignition had happened when one of the regulars heard a trader making a comment about the moleman's speed. The regular, in his oh-so-rational state, after several pints of Tugworth's Light Tugoff Ale (the joke in the name being that the ale was actually incredibly strong), had interpreted the comments as a far more serious slur about molepeople generally, and decided to rally to Chag's defence by slamming a wooden mug into the trader's face. It was the resulting scream of pain that had reminded Darl she really should get back to the bar.

By the time she appeared on the stairs overlooking the barroom, Chag was on the customer side of the bar and had the regular in a headlock. For once, the respective levels of inebriation in each party worked in Chag's favour. The regulars were too drunk to put up a real fight, having started drinking almost as soon as the bar had opened at lunchtime. The traders were yet to have their first drink, and after a long day of work were in no mood to do anything overly energetic. Thankfully, Chag's immediate intervention gave the traders the excuse they needed to not have to consider retaliation, and they moved away from the bar as the offender was rapidly hustled out of the front door. Not only that, but Chag was surprisingly intimidating and there were very few people who wanted to get involved with a fight that was likely to have him in the middle of it.

Behind the bar Chag appeared placid and unassuming, standing about four and a half feet tall, with his grey tipped black velvet hair that gave off a purple sheen in the right light. However, up close and personal the long claws and broad shoulders became his defining features, somehow amplified by the speed and ease with which he could put a six-foot tall person into a headlock.

The tension, that had been starting to ease as the groups moved away from each other, dissipated completely once Darl reached the bottom of the stairs. She smiled at the traders, apologised for the busy bar, and ushered them to a table on the far side of the barroom. A calm had descended and even the man clutching his broken nose apologised for the blood he had spilled on the floor. She then suggested to Stinky Mike, the birthday boy, that he and his friends should probably ease off on the celebrating if they wanted to stay at the Muddy Toad.

"Sorry," she said earnestly to Chag as the moleman returned from providing the man with the broken nose some clean cloths and a glass of Old Briggs Ruffest (possibly the only drink in the inn that didn't have a comedy name and was sufficiently cheap that the fiscally prudent Darl would, on occasions such as these, allow it to be given away free).

"Ah, don't worry about me," said Chag. She smiled in response. She knew she didn't have to worry about him - he could easily take care of anything the bar could throw at him - but Chag was her oldest and dearest friend, so she did.

"Where'd you get to this afternoon?" he asked in his dry, matter-of-fact voice, before appending a quick, "If you don't mind me asking?"

"I don't mind you asking," she replied. "But you'll have to wait for my answer. Truth be told I rather hoped you would ask. There's a small chance I might need to call upon your expertise in the not-too-distant future."

Chag gave an awkward smile by way of reply. As an ex-miner, an ex-furniture maker, and an ex-soldier, Chag had quite a considerable range of expertise. Now entering his early two hundreds, he felt as though he might be getting a bit past his prime, and as no furniture had been broken in the most recent bust-up, he had an inkling that the expertise she was referring to was the one he was least excited about offering.

The rest of the night passed without any further conversation on the subject, despite Darl's, and now Chag's, minds working overtime. The busy bar was a welcome distraction, and it didn't seem long before the last customers left, and the doors were locked behind them.

It was on nights like this that they would usually finish off with a quiet pint or two once all the cleaning was done and the cook had gone home. They would sit silently on the same table, quench their thirst and bask in the joy of a good job well done. But this was not a normal night and the silence that now draped itself around them was not that of exhausted fulfilment, but unspoken awkwardness. Their respective preoccupations prevented a conversation because they both knew this would crystalise their concerns - concerns which neither really wanted to acknowledge until they absolutely had to.

The silence was broken by the handle of the locked front door being turned from outside. Darl stood, welcoming the distraction. She walked to the peek hole and looked through. Gerald was outside shivering in the night air. Despite his size and solid build, the way he stood, arms wrapped around himself, uncertainty on his face, reassured her that she was doing the right thing. She began to draw back the bolts on the inside of the door. At the sound of the locks being opened, Gerald straightened himself up, pulled his shoulders back and gave the smile of someone who had found somewhere to be, and maybe even someone who might care about him.

Chag stared at Gerald as he entered the inn, and Darl gave him a brief hug. Gerald could feel Chag's eyes on him as he walked towards the table and wondered for the first time what the moleman really thought of him. Emotionally and physically exhausted, he decided that this was a worry for another time. This day was now finished for him. Sensing this, Darl put an arm around him and guided him straight up to his room.

Gerald was exhausted and sleep found him quickly that night. Somewhere in the darkness of his dreams he looked down upon himself. He was walking along the road towards the town he had walked the day before, but the town was not there. Instead, there was the burnt-out wreck of the village, desolate and deprived of its newly found fortune. He saw the faces of the mob that had chased him all those years ago, older, but still there, ghostly, and yet somehow still tangible. As he got closer to them, they started to shuffle forward. Stinking, grave-rotten breath rolled in clouds from their open mouths. Tendrils of the foetid air snaked around him, finding its way into his throat, making him gag and choke.

"Thief, thief, thief!" they appeared to chant in unison, although the words seemed disconnected and out of time with the movement of their mouths. This made Gerald think that the clamour and noise that appeared to come from the cadaverous crowd actually originated from somewhere else entirely.

Rotten eyeballs leered, torn lips opened and shut exposing broken teeth, and the closer they got to him the more carrion-like they became in appearance. They had an energy about them, a dark energy that grew with each step forward they took. It was ripe and ready to burst. It was a barely suppressed eagerness to surge forward and complete the task that they had started all those years before, but something stopped them. Something held them back, although he felt no relief at this, only the slightest notion that whatever it was that held them back did not do so for his safety, only his preservation. There was an uncomfortable feeling that something far worse wanted to get their hands on him. Something that was now in the crowd, watching him far more intently than the rest of the villagers, but he could not for the life of him see what, or maybe who, they were. And yet, despite the nightmare he continued to sleep deeply until eventually the night passed, taking with it the dream, and bringing the welcome relief that only sunlight can impart upon the world.

Chapter 6

The morning light had framed the curtains in Gerald's room with a golden glow for quite some time before he even considered getting out of bed. He had been exhausted by the time he had finally made it back to the inn the night before. So much so that even the nightmare had done little to interrupt his sleep. He had woken briefly as the zombie villagers had finally closed in on him, escaping both the dream and their grasping hands. But no sooner were his eyes open, than they closed again, and he returned to a deep slumber free from any further interruptions.

Alone in his room feeling warm and refreshed, he started to think about the events of the previous day. At first, he struggled to piece them together. It was like his memory had shattered and he was looking at the pieces of a jagged-edged puzzle that, no matter how he arranged them, would not fit back together. It didn't help that there seemed to be pieces missing. Then to add to the general confusion there also appeared to be extra pieces that looked like they were from the original picture, but when put in place changed what he thought the picture was meant to look like; not beyond recognition, but certainly enough to make him question how he remembered the day. It was as though, he thought, he had lived the day twice and now had to decide which version of events he wanted to hold on to.

In one memory he had enjoyed breakfast with Darl, and during the course of the meal she had invited him to stay at the inn. This was at odds with the alternate, and altogether less appealing, memory of the moleman jabbing him in the ribs with a broom and the smell of vomit, amongst other things, wafting from a bucket that had been left just behind the chair he had woken up in. In the afternoon his memory was divided as to whether the innkeeper had been at the graveyard or not. Gerald found it all very disconcerting. Fortunately, the mix of alcohol, emotion, and tiredness he had experienced over the past few days gave him an excuse, he was only too willing to embrace, to avoid dwelling on the issue any further. He desperately wanted to believe that this journey into the outside world did not have to be marked with the blood and pain of his previous outing. So, suppressing the feeling that something wasn't quite right, he embraced the lack of dismembered corpses around his bed as a sign that he was not in any immediate danger. He reasoned, albeit naively, that had Darl or the moleman wanted to hurt him, they had already had sufficient opportunities to do so. He pushed away his usual desire to escape, telling himself that he was safe, at least for the time being.

It briefly crossed his mind that Darl might be trying to lull him into a false sense of security, but he could not think of a reason why she would want to do that. After all they had only just met.

Confused as they might now be, the events of the previous days had gone a long way to helping him start to confront, and so begin to lay to rest, the worries and fears that had stopped him from leaving the sanctuary to make his own way in the world. Even the slaughter at the brothel was starting to feel as though it had happened a lifetime ago, which in human lifetimes it had, and he had no reason to believe he was no longer human. Anyway, he thought, it was all becoming quite academic. He had already decided that he would be leaving Spindle-Upon-Spindle just as soon as he had a hearty breakfast inside of him. So, if Darl did have any plans for him, she had about an hour or so to execute them.

As his thoughts moved onto what his final breakfast in the town should consist of Gerald heard a loud, slow knock on the door of the inn. It was accompanied by a demand to open up by the order of the Watch. The sounds echoed around the ground floor before rolling upstairs and into his ears. Intrigued, he threw as many clothes on as would allow him to meet the criteria of decent and carried the rest with him onto the landing. Crouching at the top of the stairs he listened, as the door was opened.

"What can I do for you officer?" he heard Darl say politely, albeit with an undertone that suggested she had better things to do than talking to him. Shirt on, Gerald crept downstairs.

"Go on... tell her," grumbled an old man, who stood next to the Watchman with an unnecessarily heavy-looking walking stick.

The Watchman looked slightly awkward. Although he didn't know Darl personally, he knew her by reputation. She was considered one of the better innkeepers in the town, despite many of her clientele being known a little too personally to the Watchman for petty crime, public order offences and, what Darl was widely reported to describe as, general shenanigans. On the odd occasions the Watch was called to the Muddy Toad, the incidents they were called to deal with were usually resolved by the time they arrived. The Watchmen would then promptly be dismissed by her with a smile and a friendly chorus of "You can't run a bar without breaking the odd bottle" by way of explanation.

"Tell her," the old man said again, more firmly this time.

"Tell me what?" Darl asked politely, never one to start a conversation with a Watchman on the wrong foot.

"Well madam," the Watchman said slowly and carefully. "I have been led to believe the man who burnt down the old village of Spindle is currently residing with you."

"Believe nothing. I know for a fact he's in there and he needs to face justice," the old man interjected, clearly irritated that the Watchman had not taken his word as gospel.

"Pardon?" Darl asked, feigning disbelief, because by now she was very confident that Gerald had razed the old place to the ground.

"I was here the other night when he was bragging about it," the old man said.

"Yes, I remember it. Not only did my incredibly drunk customer claim to burn down the village almost a hundred years ago, but he also spent a considerable amount of time telling us about his best friend, who is apparently a talking squirrel," Darl said flatly to the old man, careful not to sound in anyway patronising. "A man of your age and wisdom is surely well aware of just how much rubbish drunk people talk?"

"Details, woman, details," the old man said with a wicked look in his eyes, tapping his forefinger on the side of his nose. "My dad led the villagers who chased that little toerag. He saw the trees spirit him away, and that drunk told it exactly the same way my dad told me."

"So, you're saying that no one other than your dad, you, and the twelve-year-old boy he so bravely led a mob after, know what happened on that ill-fated morning?" Darl asked, not in the mood to deal with this rather strange turn of events.

"Not in that much detail," the old man spat.

Darl adjusted her gaze, she looked the Watchman directly in his eyes and said, "Officer, I've been in this town for what... oooh... maybe twenty years. In that time, I've heard that particular version of events more than a few times from different folk, including his old dad before he passed away. I also heard that the twelve-year-old boy, heroically chased by his dad's mob, outran them, fell down a ditch, got carried away in the jaws of a dark wolf, and my personal favourite, sprouted wings out of his arse and flew off. I'm not sure getting drunk and regurgitating the imaginings of bored farm labourers is really a crime, is it? Or is the policing of storytelling now part of the Watch's remit?"

"Details!" the old man shouted, before the officer could reply.

"Were you there?" Darl responded coolly, feeling there was a high likelihood the old man was about to launch into a rant which would involve the word details being used over and over again, if she wasn't careful.

"No, of course not - I wasn't even born…" the old man began.

"So, the only details you know are the ones your crazy old father told you," Darl cut in.

"What? How dare…" the old man tried again.

"Touched a nerve, have I? How dare you show up at my bar bandying around ridiculous accusations of hundred-year-old crimes at my clientele? Not only is it ridiculous, but you haven't a shred of evidence. And as for what your old man had to say…… well, everyone knows he spent his last days propping up the corners of the town's worst bars, because no other inns would have him, threatening to summon demons and bring about the end of the world. Clearly an overactive imagination runs in your family," Darl said, now unable to hide the anger building in her voice. "Just give it up."

"But…" stammered the old man, getting increasingly flustered.

Before he could continue, Darl raised a hand, and he became silent despite having very strong feelings that he still had quite a lot to say for himself. Darl shouted to Gerald, who she knew was now watching proceedings from behind the bar. As she spoke his name, the old man's eyes twitched in recognition, but he still found himself unable to give voice to the fact that the man coming to the door and the child had the same name. Gerald felt a bit sheepish as he joined Darl in the doorway, despite her valiant defence of him.

"Officer, I would like to introduce my moron nephew, who I understand shares a name with the boy we have been discussing - although I would wager not a birthday. And definitely not his age," Darl said, snapping her gaze across to the old man. "And yes, he is absolutely the sort of idiot who would move to a town, pick up on the local gossip and find some way to make an absolute fool out of himself, especially if it meant a couple of hours of attention and a free drink or two. I can only apologise if he caused you any distress. I've already taken him to task over the matter and told him that a few people in the bar that night thought his actions were in pretty poor taste."

The Watchman looked Gerald up and down, seeing an opportunity for the sort of police work he was more familiar with. He turned to the old man. "Is this the man you heard talking?" he asked.

"Yes," the old man spat between his teeth, guessing what would happen next.

The Watchman turned back to Gerald. "How old are you sir?"

"About twenty, I think. I'm not great with numbers I'm afraid," Gerald replied.

The Watchman nodded sagely. "I don't think there's anything more to be done here," he said, relieved that a situation in which he had felt completely out of his depth, for so many reasons, appeared to have resolved itself in a way that he could easily explain to his superiors; that was, if they were interested enough to ask.

The old man stood rooted to the ground in anger. His face was red, and he looked about ready to explode. He raised his stick and shook it at Gerald. "You'll get yours, you little toerag. My dad wasn't mad. He told me everything he knew. And I do mean everything. You want to see what my dad knew about demons? Well, I'll show you then," he raged before turning on his heel and storming off.

The Watchman ignored the old man's rant and subsequent retreat across the market square. He turned to Darl and apologised for wasting her time. He then checked to see which way the old man had gone before sauntering off in the opposite direction.

"Right, you, back inside," Darl said to Gerald, waving him away from the door.

Gerald shuffled back into the bar, heart pounding. "What the hell was that all about?" he asked.

"Clearly someone has a long memory and too much time on their hands," Darl said with a gravity that Gerald had not heard in her voice before.

"What was all that nonsense about demons? Was he really threatening to summon one? Silly old fool," Gerald said, desperate to move the conversation away from what he may, or may not, have done.

Darl looked at him and said, "I have no idea, but if his dad did have a direct line to a demon, then maybe he does too? I'm certainly not sitting here waiting to find out though."

"But you just said it was all nonsense?" said Gerald, suddenly feeling more than a little confused.

44

"Oh, sorry, what was I meant to say? Actually, this is the guy who set the village on fire a hundred years ago. Oh yeah, and by the way I met your dad once, and you're right - he wasn't as mad as everyone said. And he probably did know how to summon a demon," she replied, sarcasm dripping from every word.

"But... what? You think I...?" Gerald said, making a feeble attempt to protest his innocence.

"By the blood of the angels! What kind of a fool do you take me for?" Darl growled. Gerald decided this was one of those questions that it was best not to answer. "I know you started the fire, but I don't care a fig about that. To me it's an inconsequential fire in an inconsequential village. So please don't get excited about it. The reason you're here right now is because of the rose."

Gerald looked genuinely shocked. "How do you know about the rose?" he asked.

"How do you think? When you were absolutely pie-eyed the night before last, you didn't stop talking until you passed out. It wasn't just the fire you talked about. It was the rose, the brothel, the forest, even the irk," Darl replied angrily. "You just opened your mouth, and it all came out. The only saving grace of your little bid for attention was that none of my clientele ended up being chopped into little pieces. That, and you look far too young and stupid to have actually been involved with any of it, so nobody believed you."

Gerald looked shaken. It dawned on him that he maybe should have disappeared out of the window that morning after all. Darl waved Gerald onto a chair with a brusque "Sit, and don't you dare move", before disappearing off towards the kitchen. For the first time that morning Gerald properly looked at the bar around him, all set up for another busy day. Chag had already completed his morning clean. The wooden tabletops glowed as the little light that found its way in through the small windows reflected off their highly polished surfaces. The fragrance of soap and wax mingled with the smell of stale ale and smoke that permeated every fibre of the bar. He resigned himself to the likelihood that he would not be leaving that morning, and that everything he had thought was now behind him was once again firmly in front of him. At least she didn't seem to want to kill him though, he consoled himself, although deep down he knew the day was only just beginning, feelings could still change.

Darl returned moments later with a sharp "Follow me", and together they walked in silence back up the stairs. This time they went through the door that led into Darl's room.

There were three rooms on the first floor of the inn, and to maximise income Darl kept two of them empty for paying customers looking for a bed for the night. The third, and by far the largest, served as her living quarters.

As soon as Gerald walked in, he was taken back by the sheer volume of what he could only describe as stuff crammed into the room. It made him think of his own empty little hut by the lake and how it reflected his own empty little life, in stark contrast to the evidence of Darl's laid out in front of him. He was not an expert in old books or rare antiquities, yet he felt it was safe to assume that he was now surrounded by them. Either, he thought, she was well travelled, or she had spent large sums of money in the local market, which he doubted traded in the various vases, books, parchments, and knickknacks that covered just about every inch of available space.

Darl ushered him towards an expansive, but otherwise unremarkable, table that took up about a quarter of the room. Books and papers were piled high on top of it and stacked neatly underneath it. There was just enough space for him to rest an elbow on the tabletop as he and Darl sat down on a pair of ornate wooden chairs facing one another.

Ever polite, and seemingly starting to calm down, Darl offered him a cup of tea and an apology for the mess. Once the tea was made, Darl returned to her seat and an uncomfortable silence filled the room. Gerald wondered if she expected him to begin talking. Fortunately, she didn't, at least not immediately. After a few seconds she took a deep breath and began.

"I must admit I've not been entirely honest about my reasons for helping you over the past couple of days. But I want to assure you my intentions are entirely harmless. You are clearly not the sharpest tool in the box, and I'm pretty sure you're not a bad person, but I think it's fair to assume you've made some pretty poor life choices," she said slowly, weighing up each word before she spoke, and continuing before Gerald had an opportunity to protest. "I really don't know where to begin. I've been going back and forth in my head about it all since you arrived, trying to work out the best way forward and what the best thing to do is. Whether to let sleeping wolves slumber, or just put it all out there. Truth be told, I was hoping for a few more days to decide. Or maybe, really, I was hoping that you'd disappear and then I wouldn't have to have this conversation with you. Unfortunately, that old git knows exactly who you are, and if I'm completely honest I really don't need you wandering off into the world telling your bloody stories. And absolutely no one needs demons wandering around the town."

"You really do believe him, don't you?" Gerald said, reprioritising the many questions Darl's words raised, which he considered much less important now demons seemed to be a recurring topic of conversation.

"I'm a firm believer in not instantly dismissing something just because you want it not to be true. I spoke to his father just before he passed away. He would occasionally have a drink here, and as the old man is so fond of saying, there were details in his ramblings. Details he shouldn't have known unless he'd had some sort of contact with a creature from the Abyss," she explained.

"That's not good. But what has this all got to do with the rose?" Gerald asked.

"I'm hoping nothing, but I'm not a great believer in coincidences. I asked you up here because I wanted to hear your stories again. I find stories are always much better when the teller is sober and well rested," she replied. Gerald nodded, and let Darl continue. "Start from the fire in Spindle. I want to hear absolutely everything. Maybe then I can start to properly get my thoughts in order."

Now it was Gerald's turn to take a deep breath, "Everything?" he asked.

Darl's interest in the rose and old men who could summon demons gave Gerald the distinct impression he'd blundered into the sort of thing he had set out to avoid. He tried to remember why he'd thought leaving the sanctuary was a good idea but couldn't. Darl nodded a response to his one-word question, and he began.

Over the course of the next few hours, he explained to her how the fire in Spindle had started as a result of him accidently knocking over an oil lamp as he stole bread. He spoke about his narrow escape from the angry mob, his life growing up in the sanctuary, living in fear of leaving and learning to accept the loneliness. He told her about the voice that had tortured him and sent him to the big house in the city of Tanglehaven, his theft of a rose that was so seemingly straight-forward and so well paid, his celebration at the brothel and the horrific scenes he awoke to. He told her about his flight with the thing grasping at his heels, and finally his conversation with the irk that had resulted in his eventual arrival at the Muddy Toad.

47

Throughout his account Darl listened intently, nodding encouragingly when he occasionally got a little emotional, and asking lots of questions. When he had finished, he gave the smallest of smiles and once again thanked Darl for her hospitality before apologising, although he wasn't quite sure what for, but it seemed the right thing to do.

She returned the smile. "That's quite a story," she said, then stared silently into the distance for a few seconds before continuing. "Your thanks and apology are welcome. And whilst you might not believe this just now, I think your being here is probably for the best."

Gerald sat quietly digesting Darl's response, not sure he agreed with her. His tea had gone cold, so Darl offered to make him a fresh cup. He nodded, and sensing his awkwardness and uncertainty, she decided it was time to share a story with him that she had not told anyone for many centuries.

"Have you heard the story of the Rose of Amzharr?" She asked. Gerald shook his head. "Then I shall tell you. The Rose of Amzharr was the first flower. A perfect bloom grown in the Void, that would go on to become the mother and father of all flowers. Being a perfect flower, it, of course, blooms eternally. At first, when the world was new and all who lived in it were immortal, the rose was sought for its beauty, Great battles were fought so that one immortal might wrest it from the grasp of another. Eventually, though, the end of the age of the immortals came and the short-lived peoples began to populate the world.

"Whilst the immortals remained, the populations of the new races, the Kar'eens, Molepeople and Humans, started to grow. At first, the immortals ignored the new races, believing their mortality to be so great a weakness that they would never amount to anything. However, they grossly underestimated the humans in particular. As you well know, humans are the shortest-lived of all the new peoples, but unlike the immortals they did not see their momentary existence as a disadvantage. If anything, they regarded it as a challenge. Men and women looked at the immortals, and the other longer-lived races, and realised just how short their time in the world was. Rather than relax and enjoy their limited time, they instead laboured away in an attempt to create something that would allow them to grasp at the smallest grains of immortality. Some would use their talents to build great cities, create great works of art, or find other ways to shape the world around them, that their names might live on through their creations. Others, who had no talent for creation, indulged their lust for destruction

48

and sought to make their names through bloody battles and the subjugation of entire continents.

"The immortals began to see the world changing around them for the first time in many years, driven now by human ambitions rather than their own. They hoped that in time the human race would find their place in the world and settle down. But they could never quite understand that each human who tried to make their mark on the world did so for themselves, and not their race. For a human to leave their own mark on the world so that their name would be remembered throughout the ages was the closest they could come to immortality. Humans would never simply embrace the success of their forebearers. Instead, each new generation looked to build on the success of those who had gone before, or destroy it, so that their name might be greater than the greatest names of those that had been.

"Eventually the immortals grew tired of the incessant plotting and scheming of humans. Such long-lived beings would never understand the motivation of a race so fundamentally different from themselves, so they stopped troubling themselves with what the humans did. Instead, they withdrew from the parts of the world the humans inhabited. However, some humans, obsessed with their mortality, never took their eyes off the immortals. They jealously lusted after their longevity. Some spent their entire lives endeavouring to become as the immortals, even eschewing a place in the history books as a cheap and pale imitation of the prize they sought.

"One day a human perfumier named Hobb heard a story about a rose that was grown in the Void. It was said to be the first among flowers for both its beautiful bloom and alluring scent. Hobb got to thinking. If he could find the flower and create a perfume from it, he was certain that he would forever more be hailed as the greatest perfumier the world had ever known. So, he set out to see if he could find the flower for himself. How he came by it is another story for another day, but he did eventually find it. Such was its beauty that he could only bring himself to pluck a single petal from it.

"With that single petal he created a perfume so sweet and subtle that anyone who smelt it would be instantly drawn to its wearer. However, Hobb was so enamoured of his creation that he could not bring himself to share, or even sell it. After many years of wearing the perfume every day, he noticed that he had not aged. So, at the ripe old age of two hundred

Hobb was still as fresh-faced, spritely, and energetic as he had been when he had first created the scent at the age of twenty-three.

"Unfortunately for Hobb, his longevity had been observed by a sorceress who wanted to know how he had achieved such a long and healthy life. She cast a truth spell on him, and he revealed everything he knew about the rose, including its location.

"The sorceress was not as reserved as Hobb in her ambitions. She wanted immortality. She stole the rose and started to make her own perfume, but she did not care for the smell, only the amount by which she could extend her life. Eventually she started to experiment with different ingredients in an attempt to create an elixir that would not only extend her life, but make her immortal, that she might one day sit on the throne of the gods themselves.

"Somehow, she came to believe that the answer lay in infusing the blood of immortals with the rose's petals. There was one problem – the only immortals she knew of were the creators and Guardians who were so much more powerful than her. She knew she would never be able to extract even a drop of blood from them. The sorceress set out to find another source of blood. After searching high and low, she eventually discovered the lesser immortals, and in particular the nymphs. The nymphs were peaceful beings who could only see the good in people, so at first the sorceress found it easy to lure them to her home, take them prisoner and use them for her experiments. Eventually, though, the nymphs realised her true nature and they hid from her. Her depraved schemes and ambitions were forced into the light for all to see, and the sorceress no longer bothered to hide them. She preyed openly upon the nymphs without mercy using all manner of foul magics, and unleashing beasts of prey that would carry their limp and broken bodies back to her so that she might use them as ingredients in her foul enchantments.

"At the height of the slaughter, the Guardians finally stepped in. The sorceress was stopped, and her power cast to the winds. However, the victory cost the Guardians dearly, and it's said that at about that time Death, formerly but a shade, was given a body and allowed to walk the earth as he pleased. In exchange, he agreed to keep the rose and hide it for the rest of human existence."

Darl stopped talking to take a sip of her tea. The silence made Gerald nervous, so without thinking he opened his mouth in a bid to fill it.

"That's an interesting story," Gerald said quietly. "But I don't see what it's got to do with me?"

Gerald thought he saw a blue spark flash in Darl's eyes, her jaw hardened, and he got the distinct impression that something in the story she had just told had quite a lot to do with him. He cast his eyes down as his brain tried to work out what it was. A moment or so later he looked up. He wore the expression of someone who had stumbled upon an answer, only to find the question was not what he had originally thought it was, and whilst the answer remained the same, it was infinitely less appealing in its new context.

"By the blood of the angels!" he exclaimed, and then after a little further consideration, "No. It can't be."

"It could be," replied Darl. "I can't think of any other flower that would be worth dragging someone out of sanctuary to get."

"But why me?" Gerald asked. "And why is this such a big thing for you?"

"I have no idea how you got involved with this. You certainly wouldn't be my first choice if I wanted something stolen from Death, but then I suppose I hardly know you. Maybe you have some talents you've decided to hide from me," Darl replied earnestly. Gerald sat in silence trying to get his head around whether what she had said had been an insult or a compliment.

"As for me," she continued. "Well, I have something I need to show you."

She snapped her fingers. Her face suddenly cracked like a plaster cast hit by a hammer. Gerald sat up straight, eyes wide as the cracks grew and slowly, piece by piece, her face fell away. It took a while for Gerald to understand what he saw underneath. The mask hid what looked like another face, only it was much thinner and far less defined than the mask had been. The features were more suggestions of what he would have generally expected to be on a face. There were shallow indentations where the eyes should have been, with pinched flesh between them that suggested a nose, and the slightest sunken line of a mouth. Then there was the gentle blue glow that blurred the lines where the face ended and the world around it began.

"It was my people who were hunted, and butchered, so that evil witch could extend her own life," a voice growled, which Gerald assumed came from Darl's new face despite a complete lack of movement in any of her features.

Gerald remained silent and statue-still. Over the last two days his world had been blown apart. The reassuring boredom of the sanctuary had been shattered and a world of ancient stories had come to life around him. When he had started his journey to the town, he had assumed that he would be lynched by an angry mob before teatime. He had been so sure of it he had not really given any thought to what his life outside the sanctuary would be like.

Once he had arrived in the new town and realised his utter irrelevance, he had, for a brief time, felt free. He had enjoyed his first taste of ale in almost seventy years, and he had felt a spark of hope ignite inside him. Suddenly he was excited about the prospect of starting his life over again. He had smiled a carefree smile. He had drunk freely, spoken to strangers and told stories. Even his hungover awakening in the morning had the feeling of celebration about it. Now, though, a day later, he started to feel panic setting in, just as he had the last time he had woken up after a night of heavy drinking. True, there weren't literally dismembered bodies lying around him, but death once again hung in the air. He had no idea what to expect next, but he made a solemn vow to himself then and there that he would not let another drop of alcohol pass his lips ever again.

"I need to know – did you keep any part of the rose?" Darl asked, the growl gone from her voice, although there was still an edge that could slice through steel.

"What? No. The voice was very clear that the whole rose had to be delivered or I would spend eternity in huge amounts of pain," Gerald replied, a quiver in his voice, unable to take his eyes off her.

"So why are you so... old?" Darl asked.

"I don't know. I always just assumed it either had something to do with the sanctuary, or it was something to do with the voice. I did once wonder if it was part of my payment for the theft. When the voice entered the sanctuary, it put me in a lot of pain, and I barely understood most of what it was talking about, if I'm honest. It didn't exactly create a good listening environment. On the odd occasions, over the years, when I've tried to work it out, I've always ended up with more questions than I have answers for, so I just try not to think about it anymore," Gerald replied.

Now it was Darl's turn to be silent. She stood, and her clothes suddenly looked bigger on her. They sagged as they readjusted themselves to hang off her smaller frame. She paced up and down the room in thought. Gerald felt her thoughts flying around, popping in and out of his head, bringing with

52

them snatches of images of the things they had shared with each other. The silence made him feel uncomfortable.

"What are you thinking? Is there something I can do to help?" Gerald asked.

Darl raised a barely visible eyebrow and shot back in a caustic tone, "I think you've done enough already."

"Darl - I get it, I messed up, but I didn't mean for any of this to happen. I didn't have a choice, and frankly even if I did, I knew so little about this bloody rose, I still would have stolen the thing…" Gerald started pleading.

"Nonsense, you told me you had a choice. Steal the rose or die. You just weren't brave enough to make the right choice. Just like you weren't brave enough to make the right choice when you ran from the village and never came back. Evil thrives off cowards like you, and that's the problem with you humans, you're all cowards. When that sorceress butchered my people, how many humans do you think stood up to her? None. Not a single one. She held an entire continent of your people in bondage, hundreds of thousands of you, and not one person had the courage to stand against her. Instead, your people knelt before her, did what she ordered and found ways to curry favour with her that they might receive her patronage and favour," Darl raged, anger causing her skin to turn shades of orange and red that flared and flickered, making it look as though she was on fire.

"Okay, I made some big mistakes, but what if I help you? I can't change the past, although right now I wish I could. You have to believe me! I would give anything to see my mother again, just one more time. But I can't; I can't change the past. So let me help at least try and fix something?" Gerald cried in an outburst so emotionally charged it took Darl by surprise. Stupid he might be, she thought, but he was also earnest, and she could feel that he genuinely wanted to help.

"Help? What can you do to help me?" Darl spat angrily.

"I don't know, but surely something is better than nothing? And besides, you can't complain about my people not helping and then refuse my help when I offer," he said.

This stopped Darl in her tracks. The orange and reds that danced across her skin cooled to a deep purple as she considered his words. Whilst she still wasn't sure what discernible talents the lad had she knew there had to be something about him. After all, the Guardians had protected him, and they had never protected a human before. She also knew that someone would have had to have gone to a lot of trouble to track him down. There was clearly something very special about the lad, although it was very well hidden. She returned to her seat and looked at him.

"Okay, fine, but if you're going to help you must be completely honest with me. Never hide anything from me and do whatever I ask," she said.

"Of course. Can I ask a question?" Gerald ventured nervously as something occurred to him. "I stole the rose almost seventy years ago now. If it's so powerful, surely whoever I stole it for should be ruling the world by now? Or at the very least killing a lot of people somewhere? I mean, something big would be happening, wouldn't it?"

"That, or whoever you stole it for lost it. Which is what I think has happened," Darl replied.

"Sorry... so you know it's lost, and rather than looking for it you're here accusing my entire race of being cowards. Surely, if it's such a concern for you, shouldn't you be looking for it?" Gerald asked defensively.

"I didn't say I know it's lost... I said I think it's lost. At least, that's what the stories I've heard say," Darl responded, a spark of anger at Gerald's tone flaring across her face.

"Stories?" said Gerald almost laughing. "Why would anyone trust stories?"

"So now you're saying you didn't set fire to a village, you didn't steal a rose, and you didn't live under the Guardians' protection for almost eighty years?" Darl asked, anger growing in her voice. "There are very few stories without a grain of truth. The challenge is finding the grain. The old man outside this morning was right; it's all about the details."

The penny dropped and Gerald understood what Darl meant. "So, what makes you think the rose was lost? Other than there not being a current supreme overlord of the world, or whatever?"

"Do you know the Lost Lands?" Darl asked. Gerald shook his head.

"They exist on the other side of the Sea of Mists. It is a continent without trees or vegetation. It was the home of the first human to find the rose, Hobb. Back then it was green and verdant, like this continent. When the rose fell into the hands of the sorceress, she ordered her people to tear down the trees, so that the Guardians could not spy on her. This was early in her reign, before she had revealed herself for what she truly was, and the people did as she asked because they thought she was a wise and kind ruler. As her power grew, she started to become paranoid and started to suspect that the Guardians could also see her through the grass and the moss, and anything that was green. She set about purging the entire continent, removing every shred of vegetation, creating the featureless wasteland it is today. Fortunately, the Sea of Mists acted as a natural barrier, curbing her ambition to rule the world just long enough for the Guardians to find a way to take the rose back.

"After that, stories about the rose disappeared. No new ones were told and slowly the old ones were forgotten, even in the Lost Lands. However, things are never truly forgotten, and several decades ago I was passing through Tanglehaven and a new story about the rose reached my ears. It was about a prince from the Lost Lands who was consumed with lust for a peasant woman and longed to have his way with her. The woman knew the prince had no interest in her beyond her body, and so she always rejected his advances. However, this did not deter him, and he continued to pester her. To get some respite from his harassment she agreed to sleep with him if he could present her with a perfect rose.

"The next day the prince began to send her rose after rose. She rejected each one, finding at least one flaw in each flower. It is said that such was the prince's desire for her that he sent her so many roses that her family made their fortune selling them on, and even sold a number back to the prince's retainers that he then sent, once again, to the woman. Eventually there were no more roses to give, so the prince set out into the world in search of a perfect bloom that he might have missed. At an inn one night he heard the story of the Rose of Amzharr. He became determined to find the fated flower, so he could present it to the woman and claim his night of passion with her. So, the prince secured the services of a master thief, who found the rose and stole it for him. However, before the prince could present the rose to the woman, disaster struck. The prince and his entire family died in a single night. It's said that the rose then disappeared. Some say that Death killed the family and took the rose back. However, the first time I heard the story the teller said that it was the rose, and not Death, that murdered the family before disappearing."

Gerald sat in silence for a moment, gathering himself before he spoke in a weak and wavering voice on the brink of tears. "I guess I'm meant to be the master thief then?" he asked, Darl nodded. "And is any of that true? About the deaths?"

"Well, not surprisingly, I haven't had the chance to pop in for a quick chat with the current incumbent of the throne of the Lost Lands. Around that time, thought, I heard news that a new king had risen to power, and claimed that the previous royal family had succumbed to a mysterious plague. Of course, politics over there are famously bloody, so a change of ruler never comes as a great surprise," Darl explained.

Gerald started to cry. "How many more people have I killed?" he whimpered.

"If it's any consolation, royal families of the Lost Lands tend to be pretty horrible people, so I wouldn't beat yourself up too much over them," Darl said, moving closer to him and putting an arm around his shoulders.

"So, where's the rose now?" Gerald asked, wiping the tears from his eyes.

"I'm not sure anyone knows. Talking about the rose amongst immortals is generally discouraged; it's something of a taboo. And talking about the rose with mortals is not something I would normally ever do," Darl said.

"Yeah, I get why you wouldn't want to discuss it with a mortal, but why is it a taboo amongst immortals?" Gerald asked.

"I don't know. I always get the feeling that there's far more to it than I'm privy to. After all I'm only a nymph, made to be a mere minion," Darl replied. "Besides, on the odd occasion I've actually spoken with another immortal in recent years about the theft, your theft, they've immediately dismissed it as a silly human story, always saying the rose could never be stolen. I think that gave me the excuse I needed to ignore it. Of course, that all changed once you had a few pints inside you."

"Would it help if I said that I was lying?" Gerald asked.

"That's sweet, but I think the time for looking for excuses to hide behind is over," Darl said. "For both of us."

"So, what do we do next?" Gerald asked.

"I don't know. Part of me knows it would be easier to just try and forget about it all. I was doing pretty well until you popped up. Right now, though, I don't know. I think I need some time," Darl replied.

There was nothing more either of them could think to say. The silence in the room became stale quickly, and so Darl ushered Gerald out with clear instructions that he should get some rest. She then set to restoring her human face and body before joining Chag at the bar.

It was early evening when she made her way downstairs. Rain had started falling around midday and had steadily become heavier until there was surface water on the streets outside. Anywhere that wasn't cobbled was now mud. Great cold droplets fell from the sky, beating out erratic rhythms on roofs and windows, the beat increasing as time passed. Slowly the streets had cleared of people keen to get under cover. Then the little stallholders had packed up, not only because of the lack of customers, but also because of a concern that their goods would get damaged, as water found its way through canvas and around boarding hastily thrown up at lunchtime to protect against much lighter weather. Eventually, the lack of custom had resulted in even the shops closing early.

When Darl entered the barroom, Chag had already shut the door to the Muddy Toad. He and Darl sat down, each wrapping their hands around a pint of ale as though the act alone might keep them warm. Gerald's return had meant they had not got around to having the conversation they should have had the night before. Darl reflected that in the light of all she had learnt that day it was probably for the best. She told Chag everything she and Gerald had discussed. Chag listened patiently, and two hours later he let out a long, heavy sigh.

Chapter 7

As Gerald slept, he once again began to dream. He found himself back in the big house in Tanglehaven he had visited seventy years ago, that Darl believed to be Death's home. He looked around as oil lamps mounted on the walls flickered, sending shadows chasing across the ceiling. He was in what looked like a reception room of some sort. Large paintings in elaborate ebony frames hung from a white rail that ran around each wall, a metre or so below the ceiling. The paintings were of unrecognisable images in heavy shadow, a combination he realised of both the lighting in the room and the artist's intent, making it impossible for him to make out what they depicted. Furniture crowded the room, leaving little space to move around in, and opposite him there was an open glass door with empty darkness behind it.

He felt a cold breeze on his face. It wasn't unpleasant, but it irritated him sufficiently that it made him want to shut the door. He walked carefully around the furniture and placed a hand on the door handle. He was about to close it when in the darkness a soft red glow caught his eye. He stared for a moment, drawn to the gentle light that appeared suspended in the nothingness outside.

As he moved to close the door, a memory stirred in his unconscious and instead he pushed the door further open. Suddenly parts of the garden he remembered were there, visible within the darkness. A wide path of tiny yellow and white stones led away from the house for quite some distance, its end lost to view. On either side lay lush, verdant borders filled with brightly coloured flowers. It was a beautifully enticing scene, in which he found himself yearning to play his part.

He stepped out of the door and heard the crunch of gravel underfoot. He walked slowly along the broad path towards the crimson glow, some way off in the distance up ahead. He noticed that the breeze he had felt in the room had disappeared and the darkness was comfortingly warm. There was a reverence in the way that he approached the glow, knowing now what he did about the thing that he knew would be making it. He recognised the flower instantly. Even without the knowledge that Darl had imparted to him, he had known deep down that this flower was no ordinary bloom, and the temptation to take it for himself had been strong. His breathing faltered as he wondered if this dream was intended to show him that the rose was back in Death's garden, back where it belonged. A giddy excitement overcame him at the possibility, and the thought of telling Darl that there was no longer any cause for concern.

One more touch, he thought. One more touch and I can leave you forever.

He remembered how soft the petals had been. It would not hurt, he thought, to hold it one more time before he put it from his life.

One more touch, and he could forget about it all. He could move on, make something for himself, like Darl had.

He reached out and softly brushed the plump, gently curving petals with his fingers. A scent, from which all the finest scents the world had ever known had come, tickled playfully at the inside of his nose, and before he knew what he was doing, he had picked the flower.

He held it gently in both hands and gazed at it as though it was the only reason eyes had been given the gift of sight. Around him the darkness rolled in, until Gerald and the rose might as well have been the only things in existence.

A sharp pain in his hand made him wince, not only in his dream, but also in his bed. Thorns dug into the flesh of his right hand. His heart began to pound in his chest, forcing blood through his veins towards the thorns of the thirsty rose. With each heart-driven surge the rose drank, the intensity of its glow increasing with every draught it took of Gerald's blood.

He continued to stare at it, its petals unfolding further, red light illuminating his face. He was transfixed, in spite of the pain, and did not notice the pale, slender hand that reached out of the darkness and also took hold of the stem. Feeling the hand near his own, he looked up to see a thin face, dark hair cascading around it, framing it in the night. The face had emerald eyes so bright and so deep he could not help but stare into them.

Distracted from the rose by the eyes that now probed his soul, a command swam into his brain. He relaxed his grip on the flower's stem. He winced again as the pale hand yanked the flower away, causing the vicious thorns to be plucked from his flesh. Out of the darkness a body materialised as the hand drew the rose back and cradled it, just as Gerald had done. Then the person, or whatever it was, hugged it hard against their chest.

Released from the thorns, Gerald took a step backwards. The glow from the rose now eclipsed the bright green eyes, and he could see for the first time it was a woman who now caressed the flower. Her dark hair flowed down to her waist, over an elegant blue dress that seemed to blur into the darkness.

The pain in his right hand became more intense. He looked at it and saw that the puncture wounds the thorns had made were now great bloody rips in his flesh. As he raised the hand in horror, thick red liquid started to pour down his forearm and fall onto the path. The blood ran around and between the tiny stones, before soaking up into the woman's dress and eventually running over her chest to the rose.

The woman made a gasping sound as the thorns now dug into her own flesh, and through some unconscious connection Gerald thought he could hear the rose guzzling away on her essence.

She fell.

Gerald rushed to her and knelt as she lay unconscious on the ground. There was an elegant stillness in the way she lay, a euphoric smile on her thin lips. Gerald listened as the rose continued to guzzle their blood without knowing how to stop it. The woman's skin, before pale, was now white. Her body drained it began to rot, and from the darkness flies buzzed and droned. They popped into existence in the air before diving onto the body to feast. A million, minute, moving black bodies cocooned her.

Suddenly, the woman's hands shot up, scattering flies into the air, and grabbed at Gerald's bleeding arm. Nails sliced into his flesh, and he felt them. He pulled his arm back with all his might, screaming from both the pain and the exertion. The noise echoed around the garden and the inn. Somewhere in the mess of gore, the drone of the flies, and the stench of the rotting body which filled his mouth and nose, making him want to retch, he heard Darl's voice.

"By the blood of the angels," Darl shouted as she rushed into Gerald's room. She watched in horror as Gerald's body writhed about. His right arm was stretched out in front of him as though something was pulling on it. She saw blood had soaked into the sheets and blankets he now thrashed around in.

"It's a dream!" she yelled. "Wake up, dammit!"

"Help!" Gerald yelled from inside his dream, the sound finding its way back to Darl's ears, although his mouth in the inn did not move. In a state of panic, Darl watched him, unsure what she could do to help him.

Seconds that felt like minutes slipped by and she could see he was starting to tire. He was fighting back the best he could, but it was clear his energy was fading. In a desperate bid to help Darl clicked her fingers. She let her human shell crack, and fall away from her, for a second time that day. Her lithe, blue form jumped onto the bed. She wrapped herself around

60

Gerald so tightly that her glow enveloped him, and she appeared to sink inside him.

In his dream Gerald became aware of Darl's presence. She was there beside him, grabbing onto his arm and helping him to pull. A pulse of energy suddenly erupted from her. It rolled out into the dark. As it touched the now zombie-like assailant the creature flew back letting out a guttural scream. There was a flash of purple light. Gerald and Darl found themselves launched into grey mists where they fell with whispers of "I'm still free" chasing them downwards.

Darl, conscious throughout the encounter across the worlds, found herself back on the bed, still wrapped around her guest. He was unconscious, but she could see the rise and fall of his chest. He had survived for now. She was relieved, but knew he wasn't out of the woods just yet. As she disentangled herself from him, she heard a polite cough from the doorway. Chag was stood leaning against the doorframe.

"How long have you been standing there?" she snapped.

"Long enough to know you won't appreciate any jokes about all this," he said with the trace of a smile. The smile quickly faded as he looked around the room and took in the patches of black and dark red that had now spread beyond the bed and were splattered across the walls. "What on earth happened?"

"I think Gerald got to meet a dreamwalker for the first time," Darl replied. "Someone's really got it in for him."

"The old man from this morning?" Chag asked.

"Unlikely, there's a big difference between calling demons and binding dreamwalkers. I think this whole mess would be best considered over tea and toast if I'm honest. First, though, I need to make myself more presentable. Would you mind taking care of our guest and cleaning this lot up?" she asked. Chag nodded, before bustling off down the corridor to find bandages. His first priority had to be the lad's arm. He took pride in cleaning and garnered a certain amount of satisfaction from seeing people's reaction to a job well done. Given the mess the lad had made, Chag was damned if Gerald was going to be allowed to die before he was able to appreciate the results of the hard work the moleman had ahead of him.

Gerald came to sometime around mid-morning. The dream had been so vivid and seemed so real his mind had retained each and every detail, as well as an awareness that somehow the struggle had been played out in both his dreams and his bed at the same time. When he returned to consciousness, he did so with a great deal of anxiety. He opened his eyes dreading the blood-soaked scene he expected to find. The realisation that his wounds had been neatly bandaged, that there were clean sheets beneath him, and warm blankets on top of him was a welcome surprise. His throbbing hand and a pounding headache were now the only evidence of the events of the previous night. He sensed Chag's handiwork.

As he looked around, he noticed a small wooden stool had been placed next to the door with what looked like a set of clean clothes and his knife resting on top of them. The ageing black trousers and shirt he had taken off the night before, left in a scruffy pile by the bed, were nowhere to be seen. He felt weak from the blood loss and the night's exertions, so he rose slowly, determined to find out if Darl had been injured. First, he sat upright. Then, after taking a few breaths, he turned to allow his legs to fall over the side of the bed so his feet could find the floor.

He pushed himself up to standing and walked slowly to the stool, where he gave the new clothes a onceover. He smiled as he unfolded them. There were boots and trousers in relatively inoffensive shades of brown. The shirt was red and there was a coarse, grey jacket that looked as though it would keep the cold of a bad winter at bay. He gingerly started to get dressed, being careful to avoid letting anything catch on his bandaged hand.

Fully clothed, he made his way down to the bar. The smell of toast and bacon met him on the stairs, followed by the low hum of Darl and Chag talking. The events of the night, and his conversation with Darl the previous day, had allayed the few concerns he had about the danger the innkeepers might present to him. The savaging he had received in his dreams meant that he now fully shared Darl's concerns about the rose and where, not to mention with whom, it had found itself. Carefully he walked through the final door that led to the main bar where Darl and Chag sat eating their breakfast.

"You're up!" Darl exclaimed, back in her human shell, a look of relief on her face.

"Yeah, I guess I am. Thank you, both of you. I think it's fair to say I wouldn't be here without your help," Gerald said weakly.

"No problem," Chag replied flatly.

"Can either of you explain what happened?" Gerald asked, delicately lowering himself into a seat at the table.

"Dreamwalker," Chag replied.

Gerald nodded slowly, waiting for the moleman to expand on his answer. When it became apparent no further information would be forthcoming, Gerald asked the question again, this time directing it to Darl in the hope that she would be able to furnish him with a more helpful response.

"Dreamwalkers are wild shapeshifters that inhabit the Greylands," she replied.

"And the Greylands are…?" Gerald asked before Darl had the chance to continue her explanation.

"The Greylands are, loosely speaking, where you go when you dream. Generally, it's a benign world and the dreamwalkers are harmless. Unfortunately, the right sort of power-crazed maniac with the right human organs to sacrifice can change that for one lucky person. At least for a little while anyway," Darl explained.

"I'm guessing that was the old man's demon then?" Gerald asked.

"Chag wondered if that might be the case as well," Darl replied. "I'm not convinced. It is far easier to call a demon than it is to bind a dreamwalker. Gaining entry to the Greylands alone is beyond the ability of most sorcerers. When the old man talked about demons, I'm certain he meant demons."

"So, every time I sleep, I'm risking my life?" Gerald asked, sounding scared and frustrated.

"I don't think you need to worry too much about your sleep," Darl said calmly. "From what I understand binding a dreamwalker is a pretty time-consuming process and requires quite a few specialist ingredients. It's definitely not something someone would be able to do too often. And, of course, whilst you're under my roof I'll always be on hand to help."

Gerald found Darl's response surprisingly reassuring. He relaxed a little and his brain moved onto his next pressing question, "So who else could have sent it?"

"Annoyed any wizards recently?" Chag asked.

"Not that I know of," Gerald replied in a shaky voice. "Although, I'm not sure I've ever met any."

"That's one of the dangers of getting drunk and sharing your life story with a bar full of people you've never met before," Darl said. "You never know who is going to take an interest, or why."

Gerald blushed at Darl's pointed, yet he felt entirely justified, response.

"I think the one thing we can say with any sort of certainty is that it had something to do with the rose," she continued. "Personally, I think the sooner we find it the better, for all of us."

Both Chag and Gerald gave slow nods of agreement to Darl's supposition, although their faces wore expressions that showed a clear reluctance to want to discuss the topic any further. Gerald's eyes darted around in an attempt to avoid looking at either of the innkeepers, eventually coming to rest on the food. The sight of the food reminded Gerald that he was starving and, embracing the distraction, he allowed his stomach to take over. He surveyed the meal they had laid out. There was enough, he thought, to feed the bar's clientele on a busy night. In the middle of the table was a big plate of bacon, toast, sausages, fried eggs and mushrooms that they had been working their way through. There was a spare plate and fork, which he assumed had been left for him, so without asking he grabbed them and started to pile food onto the plate. After the night he'd had, this was exactly what he needed.

The distraction proved to be short-lived as the atmosphere around the table continued to push down on them. Gerald shovelled bacon into his mouth, all the while watching Chag and Darl exchange a series of furtive glances until, eventually, she turned to him and spoke.

"How are you feeling about everything else?" she asked, before attempting to clarify her question. "About everything we discussed yesterday."

Gerald's stomach lurched; a forkful of food stopped halfway to his mouth, before being returned to his plate. He was beginning to realise his capacity to avoid confronting things which needed to be confronted was even greater than he had first thought.

"Yeah, fine," he lied, keen to avoid them for a bit longer if it was at all possible, although he suspected that Darl was not about to let him get away with that.

"Okay, if you say so, that's good," Darl replied. She gave a sigh, which Gerald took to mean that she didn't entirely believe him, before continuing, "We've been talking, and we think the time has come for all of us to make some difficult decisions."

Chapter 8

It started in the kitchen. Careless embers knocked from the fire, as Chag locked up for the night, that found some scraps of paper with which to feed their tiny glow.

An odd atmosphere pervaded the bar that day. Chag knew much of it was down to Darl. Her true nature meant she constantly threw out energy into the world that people interpreted in any number of different ways based on their own circumstances at the time. When she was calm and happy, it was at worst benign, and at its best it drew people together, helped them smile a little more easily and enjoy each other's company. However, the events of the last two days and the plans they had laid that morning had sparked a flare of emotions within her that were beyond her control. As a result, everyone in the bar had felt more than a little on edge. Customers who were usually chatty sat silent, whilst those with dark secrets and hidden pasts couldn't quite shake the feeling they were being watched by someone they had wronged. It had resulted in a quick turn over of customers and an empty bar by about nine o'clock that evening. Darl hadn't worried that her customers might identify her as the source of the negativity, which seemed to have infected the usually excitable and bubbly clientele of the Muddy Toad. She knew that only the most skilled magicians and sorcerers would have been aware that the charged atmosphere emanated from the rosy-cheeked innkeeper bustling about her business, her long auburn hair loose and emerald eyes sparkling. Fortunately, the Muddy Toad was not known for having an academic clientele, let alone a magically gifted one.

In the past two days, Darl's world had been thrown into disarray. She had gone from her happy routine looking after her business and customers, to coming face to face with the man who had stolen an artifact soaked in the blood of her people. He had taken it from a place of relative safety and released it into the world. She felt annoyed with herself for ignoring the stories that had started to resurface over the last few decades. But the truth was she had not wanted to believe that the Rose of Amzharr had escaped into the world. Or that at some point someone might come looking for her. Not because she was a threat to them, but simply because she was who she was. It was the blood of her kind that was an essential ingredient in a recipe that allowed the selfish and power-hungry to impose themselves on the world for just that bit longer than nature intended. However, confronted with Gerald, and the quickly growing list of people who seemed to want him dead, she could no longer dismiss the stories. Regardless of where the rose was physically at that moment, Gerald's adventures meant it had returned to the consciousness of humans, and that meant it was only a matter of time before someone discovered its secrets. With the catalyst of the whole messy business now residing in her spare room, she could no longer ignore it. Action had to be taken so that she could feel safe again and didn't have to spend the rest of eternity looking over her shoulder.

The first step to making that happen was to find out where the rose was. Gerald's dream had made the need to do something that much more immediate, but where did you begin to look for something that had an entire world to hide in? They had decided the best way to proceed would be to rule out the slim possibility that the rose was where it should have been.

This was, of course, no easy task. One does not casually knock at Death's door and invite oneself in for a quick chat. It generally happens the other way around. There was one thing in their favour though: most people didn't know someone who had been inside his home and survived. So, she reasoned, they should be able to find Death's home far more quickly than the rose. Of course, then there was the small matter of getting an honest answer out of a being who had no reason to give one, or indeed any answer at all. That created a whole raft of other problems, but they were problems for another day. After all, as Chag had said, there was no point in worrying about getting pricked by a needle you were searching for in a haystack, if you could not first find the haystack it was in. However, if, and she knew that this was highly unlikely, they found that the rose was with Death, then her problems were solved, and she and Chag could return to their much-loved quiet little lives.

As she and Chag had talked in the evenings and early mornings as Gerald slept, other issues had started to arise. After the hunts and the slaughter of her race, she had never felt comfortable revealing her true form to anyone she did not fully trust. Unsurprisingly, trust was not something that came easily to her. Whilst she knew the world in general would be accepting of her, the connection between her race and immortality had been forged. She did not want to encourage those few who sought life eternal to see if it could be achieved at her expense, with or without the rose. Consequently, she had adopted the disguise of the cheery innkeeper and moved every ten years or so to avoid people raising questions about her ageing, or rather lack of it. Hiding amongst humans made a long lifespan something that attracted attention, and that was the last thing she wanted. However, both Darl and Chag had enjoyed their time in Spindle-Upon-Spindle a little too much. The town had been so welcoming to them, and the Muddy Toad had become something of an institution amongst those who walked through its doors. They had become comfortable, and twenty years on from their arrival not a single discussion had been had about moving on.

Chag put it down to his age. He was not old by moleman standards, but far from a spring chicken. He reluctantly admitted to Darl that travelling and restarting his life over and over again no longer held the same appeal it once had. For the first time in a long time, he had built a series of tunnels under the inn that he now called home. He had started to become attached to the busy little market town, so had not wanted to be the first to raise the subject of leaving it. Despite that he agreed that, rose or no rose, the time had probably come for them to move on, which made the first part of the plan just about palatable to him. Although he had greater reservations than Darl about asking Death if he still had the rose, he conceded the logic behind the overall idea was sound, so the plan, at least in principle, had been agreed.

Darl did not require the extra push the duration of their stay in the town added. The attack on Gerald the night before was enough, and as Gerald had rested that morning, she had convinced Chag that the date of their departure had to be brought forward. It had to be that evening.

The attack had panicked her, not because she was worried about Gerald; he was nice enough, but not exactly what she would describe as a close friend, or even a casual acquaintance. She had, though, decided to forgive him for his role in the theft of the rose after Chag had, unexpectedly, come to his defence. The moleman had theorised that if someone had wanted the rose so badly, they would have eventually found someone willing to steal it. If it hadn't been Gerald, it would have been someone else. Of course, it helped that neither of them could understand why Gerald had been chosen for the job. He certainly didn't seem to have any of the qualities you would associate with the sort of person who could break into the home of one of the great immortals and get out again alive. Because of this she was happy to take the view that he had been a victim of circumstance. Although they reminded each other that there were a lot of things about him that weren't quite as they should have been, so - master thief or not, forgiven or not - he still needed watching.

Darl's real concern was that she had entered Gerald's dream. That meant there was a chance that if whoever had unleashed the dreamwalker was hanging around in the darkness, they might have seen her. Consequently, they would know that there was at least one nymph left in the world, something she had done her best to hide for so long.

Flames started to sprout from the tiny bits of paper and danced their way to a small puddle of oil, growing, before reaching up to take hold of a cloth that hung from a table. They then spread across the floor and up the walls of the timber-framed building. It wasn't long until the Muddy Toad was engulfed in flames. Cries of "FIRE!" echoed around the streets. Bells rang, and dots of light from the Watchmen's lanterns moved rapidly through the sleeping town, converging on the inn.

Gerald's misadventures all those years earlier had a lasting impact on the people of Spindle. As the town had grown under the watchful gaze of its elders, they had insisted the Watch should be as practised in putting out fires as they were in the apprehension of criminals. Fortunately, they were far better at dealing with fires, and it did not take long for chains of bucket-passers to be formed of citizens who had been fast asleep only a few seconds before. In a matter of minutes Spindle-Upon-Spindle was awake, and rather than look for someone to blame, the citizenry flew into a flurry of activity, directed by the officers of the Watch, to get the fire under control and prevent it from spreading to nearby houses.

Jade stood watching the dancing flames. She normally enjoyed a good fire, particularly when it was someone else's stuff, or just someone else, in the middle of it. This fire was, however, a decided inconvenience. She looked on from the other side of the market square as the Watch and the townsfolk did their best to contain it. Annoyed by the timing, she was tempted to use the little magic she had to give the fire a nudge over towards a nearby shop but thought better of it. There were already more people than was helpful milling around, and she had a headache.

The headache had been caused by the "summoning", as humans liked to call it. She was always amazed by the heights upon which humans perceived themselves to rest, despite their fragility and obvious limits. Summoning was, to Jade, the perfect example of just how short-sighted humans could be when evaluating their place in the world. In the minds of most humans, summoning was about enslaving a demon and binding it to their will. In reality, it was more of a very long-distance tap on the shoulder, followed by a "get over here" through time and space. There was certainly no enslavement involved, and no amount of dressing up in robes, or drawing pretty patterns in condiments on the floor, was going to protect a human from the wrath of a demon who had just had their afternoon nap interrupted.

Jade considered it to be one of the more unusual, not to mention annoying, aspects of demonhood. However, in a weird way, that only evolution could explain properly, if evolution could talk, it kind of made sense. Most people turned to summoning because they were desperate for something and that meant, after the initial realisation that the summoner was not in control of the situation, there was usually a deal to be done very much in the demon's favour. So, whilst the timing was invariably inconvenient, there was a fruitfulness to it that most demons, including Jade, saw as broadly beneficial.

As she had stepped out of the swirling portal that afternoon, to be confronted by the angry old man with the big stick ranting about villages being set on fire, the thought of making him her dinner had flashed through her mind. She had smiled her best "I'm gonna eat ya" smile as she walked casually through the salt circles intended to bind her, tail shooting out from behind, wrapping itself around his neck and jerking him off the ground. Then he had started warbling about someone called Gerald, and the name rang a bell.

"Is this Spindle?" she enquired, dredging her memory.

"Yes," the old man gasped, grabbing at the tail in a vain attempt to loosen her grip.

"Intriguing. So, that would make you the son of the old busybody who promised to contact me when Gerald returned to the village?" she guessed, factoring in the lifespan of humans with the striking similarity of the man's face to the man she had originally engaged to watch for the lad's return.

"Yes," the old man gasped.

"So where is he?" she snapped.

"The Muddy Toad," he responded.

"Thank you," she replied.

Jade then tied the man to a chair as he rambled on about how she should have more respect, and that she was meant to be serving him. Before Jade left the old man's house, but away from where he could see, she morphed into her human form. She had chosen it to set people at ease and instil in anyone wanting to attack her a tremendous amount of overconfidence. So, half an hour later a short, fragile-looking woman with white hair, in her early fifties, made her way to the bar of the Muddy Toad and ordered a cup of tea. The bar was poorly lit and there was an atmosphere that suggested a fight might break out at any moment, exactly the sort of bar she loved. As Jade pretended to totter from the bar to a table, cup of tea shaking in her hands, she pondered the bar staff. An oldish moleman had served her, which was unusual. They were generally a solitary race who tended to opt for jobs with far less people contact. The barmaid, however, was exactly the sort of person she would have expected to see bustling around in an establishment like this. The clientele looked, by and large, miserable. Except for those who sat alone in small booths around the edges of the room staring into the distance, facial expressions somewhere between hunted and haunted. It didn't surprise her that Gerald had ended up in a place like this.

She stayed for as long as she thought was reasonable for an old lady to finish a cup of tea without arousing suspicion, which in all universes is an inordinately long time. She looked around for any signs of her quarry. Her patience was eventually rewarded with a fleeting glimpse of Gerald, right arm heavily bandaged, closing a door that had a large "private" sign hung on it.

She smiled what she thought was a sweet old lady smile and drained the final drops of tea from her cup, before leaving the bar to collect her tools. She dispelled any ideas she had that the lad's damaged hand might make things easier for her. The last time they had met he had been unconscious, and he had still managed to evade her. This time, though, she knew he was an immortal, and she knew where to find the right tools for the job. She walked back across the market square, heading towards the smallest-looking streets which eventually turned into the dark and undesirable alleys that every town has, where no one who anyone will take too seriously spends any time. Away from the prying eyes of those who might be believed, she returned to her demonic self. Green skin stretched over solid muscles, wings sprouted from her shoulder blades, clawed hands and feet revealed themselves, a thick tail almost as long as she was tall appeared, and bony spines sprouted from her forearms. She flew straight up into the sky before heading to the place where she had hidden what she would need all those years ago, just in case.

As she flew, she replayed the events in Tanglehaven and then the chase through the forests, back to the sanctuary. It was a strange job, she remembered. It had started out like any other. Someone had made her an offer to kill someone else. As was so often the case, there was no explanation given as to why the murder was required, and Jade was never one to be overly bothered about details. She had been led to believe, though, that Gerald was a mortal. If had turned out to not be the case, which meant she had not had the tools on hand to complete the job. This was unfortunate for her, and very unusual in her experience for an employer not to know something as important about the target as that. What was more unusual, though, was that not only had her fee been paid up front when the agreement had been made, but no evidence of the completion of the job had been requested. This was unheard of, but it was a situation she was, at the time, only too happy to be in. It became even more convenient when the lad went to ground in the sacred grove, putting himself beyond her reach. She had been frustrated at the time that she had been unable to complete the job, but when she received no further contact from the client she soon forgot about Gerald and moved onto her next contract. On balance, she thought, being called back to Spindle was probably for the best. She would be able to finish what she had started, so if the client did ever resurface there would be no awkward conversations or requests for refunds.

Later that evening, watching the flames leap higher and the streets become busier, she cursed Gerald under her breath. Had he actually managed to escape her once again? There was a chance, she supposed, that this had been an accident and he was trapped in the building. If that was the case, the flames wouldn't kill him, but with all the people milling around, now was not the time for her to go walking into an inferno to have a nose around. She morphed back into her human form and tottered back to the old man's house. Coincidence? She hoped so.

Jade had never liked the concept of coincidence. The idea that certain things just happened because they did, had never really sat well with her. That wasn't the way the world worked. Things happened, and then other things happened. The great galactic domino effect connected the present to the past and each event to the one that preceded it. That was the way the world worked. Her arriving on the same day that Gerald's current home went up in smoke stank to high heaven of something that just wasn't right. She thought for a minute. If the old man had been angry enough at Gerald's return to summon her, and he had been very angry, maybe someone else in the village was just as angry but didn't have a demon to bother. She remembered he had been rambling on about fires at the point her tail had slipped around his neck. Maybe she should have spent a bit more time listening to him?

"Well, there's no time like the present," she said out loud to the night sky.

Chapter 9

"I had nothing to do with it," the old man choked, still bound to the chair, only now both he and the chair hovered above the ground, held there by Jade's tail which was once again wrapped around his neck. "I summoned you to deal with him. Why burn down the inn? Besides, I've been tied up here all afternoon."

"Know anyone who might have?" Jade spat. "Are there any other members of the Let's Avenge The Hundred-Year-Old Crime Club I should know about?"

"No. It's just me," the old man struggled to say.

"Figures. It's usually sad loners like you who call me in to do their dirty work. I suppose if you actually had some mates, you might have managed to find enough balls between you to sort him out yourself," Jade growled, lowering him to the ground and releasing her tail. "But just to be absolutely sure, because you are so sad and pathetic, I'll count to ten and I'll give you one last chance to tell me about anyone else who might have had a reason to burn that inn down."

"What happens after you reach ten?" the old man asked, sounding terrified.

"I'll hurt you," Jade leered, teeth bared.

"But there isn't anyone else, I swear," he shouted in desperation.

"Okay then," Jade said sweetly. "I'll believe you, but you have to promise on your life."

"Thank you," the old man gasped, tears of relief starting to well up in his eyes. "I prom…"

There was a loud snap as Jade's tail lashed out, catching him full in the face with a blow that spun his head around and left it looking behind him. "Not at all," she replied. She sighed. The interrogation had been tough on her, having to listen to all that nonsense about the village being burnt down, but at least it explained why his father had been so keen to help her.

As Jade decided on her next move, Gerald watched the fire at the inn being brought under control from the scrappy grassland outside the town where the sheep now slept.

"You were right," he said to Chag. "They really do know how to manage fires now."

"Told you," the moleman said with a wink. "We would never have done it if we thought it would put anyone in any real danger. The town's been good to us."

When Chag and Darl had shared their plan with him that day, the events of almost a hundred years ago had come back to haunt him immediately. He had argued they should just pack up and leave quietly. Darl agreed that it would be preferable to leave the inn in one piece, but they couldn't be absolutely sure that there wasn't anyone watching them, especially since Gerald had managed to attract so much attention since his arrival. The fire would not only provide a distraction to anyone spying on them, she explained, but would also temporarily block the entrance to Chag's tunnels which they would use to escape through. With luck, anyone chasing after them would waste their time trying to find a trail from the inn, or through the town's streets, that wasn't there to be found. Wounds from the dreamwalker still fresh in his flesh, Gerald reluctantly agreed to the plan.

As they had made their way through Chag's tunnels, Gerald had been pleasantly surprised, although there had been no time to stand around admiring them. He hadn't been sure what to expect, but their neat orderly nature reflected their architect, and for some reason this reassured him that everything Chag and Darl had told him to address his concerns about setting the fire was true. The only thing that had bothered Gerald had been the height. He was quite a bit taller than the moleman and so the going had not been as easy as he would have liked due to the low ceilings, but he was never going to voice that particular concern to Chag.

In the fresh night air Chag gave Gerald a nudge with the staff he was carrying. "Keep moving, lad," he said, trying to distract Gerald from what was happening in the town. "Don't you worry about what's behind. We need you focused on what's ahead."

As Gerald snatched a last glimpse of the town, his concerns about the fire and the people of Spindle-Upon-Spindle ebbed away. Another feeling was growing in its place. It was the feeling that one of the unfinished chapters in his life was now closed. The little of Spindle-Upon-Spindle he had seen he had liked. So, despite his misadventures in Spindle, his Spindle, the village had clearly moved on, and it was time for him to do the same. He turned his back on the town and looked at Darl, who stood waiting for him a few meters away further up the field. "Come on," she said. "We need you to show us the way." He smiled and started to walk towards her. He felt a surge of excitement about the journey ahead, even though he knew much of it would be uphill.

As the dawn began to break, Jade mooched around the burnt-out remains of the Muddy Toad. Much of the inside of the building had been destroyed, although the frame seemed to remain largely upright, for the time being at least. In her human form, carrying the old man's unnecessarily heavy stick, she poked at the piles of ash and burnt furniture. She wondered why the innkeeper, whoever he was, was not there trying to find anything that might be salvageable, or protecting the remains from looters and inquisitive old ladies. Her experience told her that usually when businesses burnt down, anyone with a financial interest tended to make themselves known pretty quickly, regardless of the time of day. There was, of course, a chance the owner had died in the fire, but Gerald wouldn't have. He would have been able to help anyone else in the building get to safety. Unless, of course, he had done a runner once again.

Questions swam around in her head, searching for answers. What if the moleman was the innkeeper, she thought. She walked to one corner of the inn and started to move systematically around the floor, prodding at the floorboards she could get to with purpose. After a few minutes of concentrated effort, she knelt down and started scraping away ash and chunks of burnt wood. A metal handle appeared. She cleared more debris. She found a thin gap running around the handle, creating a circle just under a metre in diameter. She pulled at the handle and the door lifted. She was not surprised to see a ladder leading down into a dark room below. Noticing the ceiling of the room was quite low, she remained in her human form and began to climb down. As expected, this was what the moleman called home. The room turned out to be reasonably large, with a number of doors set into the walls. She opened each door one by one and found a series of small but comfortable living spaces, including a kitchen, some bedrooms and a bathroom. The tunnel had clearly been established for a while, and as she would expect from a moleman solid timber supports and boarding had been used to keep both the building above and the home below stable.

As she searched each room, everything seemed to be in good order, and she started to get a feel for the barman, who she now presumed to be the innkeeper. There was little in the way of personal items, which was not unusual. Molepeople were very pragmatic and placed little value on sentiment. She found a small box in a drawer filled with coins and medals that told of travel and a distinguished military career, also not surprising, as molepeople made excellent soldiers. Then she came across the curtain. It was a big, heavy, black curtain that looked quite out of place in the underground home. She thought it highly unlikely that there would be a window behind it, but she wondered if it might hide clothes or weapons, given the moleman's military background. She pulled it back to reveal a studded door with a silver handle and a keyhole beneath it. She twisted the handle and wasn't overly surprised to find it locked. She knelt and put an eye to the keyhole. There was what looked like a tunnel behind it. Pieces of the puzzle seemed to be falling into place quite quickly now.

She guessed that this would be the moleman's tunnel to the outside world, and the route by which Gerald and the moleman could have made their escape from the burning building. She reached into her shoulder bag, which looked comedically large for such a petite, old lady. She pulled out a small metal ball and stuffed it under the door. She muttered a few words in the language of the Abyss and the metal ball sent a pulse of energy directly upwards. It splintered the wood and left a huge crack that ran all the way from the bottom to the top of the door, with smaller cracks branching out to the left and right. Then she took a small mace from her bag and smashed away at one half of the door until it finally gave way to reveal a beam that had been thrust across the tunnel side of the door. This was why she didn't believe in wasting time picking locks. Anything worth anything always had several layers of protection that generally yielded far quicker to brute force than subtlety. She continued to break her way through the door until there was sufficient space for her to clamber through, retrieving the small metal ball as she went.

She now knew she was on the right track - doors to the outside world locked on the inside. The fact that someone had gone to the effort of placing a beam across the door not only meant that they didn't want people following them, but that they were concerned that people might try. She felt quite smug as her position on coincidences seemed to be confirmed once again. The fire had clearly been planned. The next question though was why?

As much as she liked the idea of Gerald running scared from her once again, it didn't quite make sense. She didn't think that anyone had recognised her that afternoon and the old man, as she understood it, had been making his threats the morning before. Surely if Gerald had actually believed the old fool, he would have left sooner, and on his own. She didn't pretend to be an expert on the behaviours of mortals, but she was pretty sure that the decision to burn down your home and business was not one that was taken lightly. So why had the moleman done it? And what was Gerald's part in all this? She pushed the questions away; now was not the time to think about something that she knew she had no answers for.

She walked slowly through the tunnel. There were tracks that indicated more than one person had passed along it recently, so she was confident that there was a chance Gerald had been one of them. She moved cautiously, checking for traps; after all, if they'd made time to get a bloody great beam into the tunnel to bar the door, it was reasonable to expect them to have taken other steps to deter anyone who might come after them.

Forty-five trap-free minutes later she found the end of the tunnel. A ladder was propped up against the earthen wall that marked its end. She climbed up and found herself in the middle of a sprawling bush which she then had to wrestle her way out of. She swiped at the branches with a cleaver she had also been carrying in the shoulder bag, and eventually found herself in the fresh air looking down on the town as the morning sun sat low behind it. She stood on the scrappy grassland Gerald and his friends had stood on only hours before, scanning the horizon in every direction just in case she was not as far behind them as she suspected.

When it was clear they were not within sight, she squatted and looked carefully at the ground studying each and every indentation. After a few seconds she found what she was looking for. The footsteps of two people had made their way from the tunnel towards the hills and the forests that crowned them in the far distance. She followed them a little way before her hunter's instinct kicked in. She remembered the path. She had walked it once before in the opposite direction. That time she had come from the sanctuary to the town in the hope that she could enlist someone to watch for Gerald's return. She congratulated herself on her choice of small-town simpleton. Managing to choose someone with so much pent-up hate for Gerald that he had passed the task onto his son, was something of a coup in her mind. Summoning might have been, on so many levels, an inconvenience, but it certainly had its uses.

Faded memories refreshed themselves and she started to stride towards the hills that would lead, she remembered, to the sanctuary. The thought of transforming into her demon body and flying crossed her mind, but the unanswered questions about what else Gerald might be fleeing from made her uneasy about breaking the cover of her human disguise. She had sufficient self-awareness to understand that the sight of an elderly lady striding through the wilds with an oversized shoulder bag and walking stick was likely to raise an eyebrow or two. But if something else was chasing her quarry, it might be keeping an eye on her as well. She wasn't going to give away any more about herself than she absolutely had to until she knew what it was, and more importantly what it might think of her.

By the time Jade was climbing the first of the hills Gerald, Darl and Chag were sat by the lake in the sanctuary, just down from his little hut. As soon as they had crossed the threshold, Darl had divested herself of her human shell. Her body glowed with a turquoise hue. She had her feet in the water and all the living things in and out of the lake had taken an instant interest in her. Insects had buzzed around her, a brave humming-bird had alighted on her shoulder, and Gerald had noticed deer and foxes watching her from a distance much closer than they had ever inspected him from. The attention had not lasted long, and the creatures had quickly returned to their respective preoccupations, but there was clearly a mutual appreciation between Darl and the local wildlife. Although the creatures' attentions were no longer on the nymph, Darl's presence seemed to embolden them, and for the first time in all the years he had been there, Gerald watched a pair of young otters frolicking in the shallows of the lake less than a metre from her toes.

"Oh, by the angels... it can't be!" came a high-pitched gasp from a nearby tree, alerting them to Joggle's presence. They looked around in unison as the irk shot down the trunk of the tree he had been sleeping in and ran towards Darl. He stopped just a few paces from her, pulled himself up to his full height, puffed out his chest and took a deep bow.

"M'lady," he said.

"Joggle!" Darl replied, voice ringing with joy. "Gerald has told me so much about you."

"Then, with your kind approval, I would like to offer you my most humble service," Joggle said, finally rising from his bow. "It has been so many years since I last saw one of your kind and, might I add, one so beautiful."

"You flatter me, Joggle," Darl responded. "It has also been a while since I last clapped eyes on one such as yourself. How is it to be an irk in the days of the mortals?"

"Thrilling, m'lady, simply thrilling. So much change, so much innovation, so much wonderment," he replied. "I would ask the same question of you, but I am only too aware of the fate of your people. Are you able to offer me any hope that the world might once again benefit from the tender care of the nymphs?"

"Unlikely, my little friend," Darl replied, the joy gone from her voice, her colour losing its vibrancy and her head dropping slightly. At the same time Gerald noticed the temperature around the lake seemed to fall slightly and the otter cubs ceased their games and swam away.

"Sorry, I probably shouldn't have mentioned the past," the irk said, also noting the change in temperature.

"Not to worry, my little friend, the past has passed. The future is my only concern at present," Darl replied. Joggle looked quizzical.

"It is possible the Rose of Amzharr is free once more." Darl answered in response to the irk's unspoken question.

A look of shock appeared on Joggle's face. "What? How?" he exclaimed.

If there was a single image, in Gerald's view, that best summed up the seriousness of the situation, it was the sight of Joggle floundering for something to say.

"Turns out I actually have a story to tell you," Gerald said to Joggle, turning red with embarrassment whilst trying to find a direction to look in that avoided having to acknowledge the stares of disapproval from the others, which now seemed to accompany the merest mention of his misadventures.

"What's all this got to do with you?" Joggle asked, turning to the lad.

"I might have stolen it," Gerald said sheepishly.

"What? When?" Joggle exclaimed, completely unaware that Gerald had ever left the forest. "I thought you'd been here pretty much all your life?"

Before any more words were spoken, Chag got to his feet. "All in good time," he said, sensing an impending discussion that was likely to impinge on his need for food. "The point in us coming here was so we could get a bit of rest without shouty old men and dreamwalkers trying to get their hands on the lad. So, before we get into swapping stories, let's get some breakfast sorted out, and then a bit of sleep for those of us that need it. There'll be plenty of time for tales afterwards."

"Dreamwalkers?" Joggle gasped.

"Apparently so," Gerald replied, raising his bandaged hand.

Despite Joggle's demands to know everything immediately, there was a general murmur of agreement that food was a higher priority. Gerald and Chag prepared a much-needed meal from what was left in his hut and the food they had brought with them. Joggle, who was never far from a nut, reclaimed his current snack and returned to gnawing away on it. Darl, empowered by her arrival in the sacred enclave, and so needing neither sleep nor food, began to tell Joggle everything that had happened whilst Gerald had been in Spindle-Upon-Spindle, and what he had told her about the theft of the rose.

As she came to the end of the story, Joggle inquired as to what they intended to do next, and an awkward silence descended on the group. Darl looked at Chag. The moleman, his usual stoic self, seemed not to make any kind of movement that Gerald could discern. Darl took this as an agreement from the moleman and started to share their plan with Joggle, who proceeded to invite himself to join them.

As Gerald watched the muted exchange between Darl and Chag, then listened as Darl told the irk about their plan, he felt for the first time that he wasn't really part of the group; at least not in the way he wanted to be. The way that Darl had taken it upon herself to tell his stories, and the way she had told them, made him feel as though she thought he was a stupid child who needed her and Chag to fix his mistakes. The feeling burnt away at him as he felt his right hand throb, reminding him that it was his life that really seemed to be the only one that was actually in any danger. Listening to the plan again, he realised that it didn't really address that; it was all about finding the rose, rather than trying to stop whoever was trying to kill him. To everyone's surprise, Gerald stood up and walked away from the group, heading around the outside of the lake, without a word to anyone.

"What's up with him?" Joggle asked.

"No idea," Darl lied, pretty sure she knew exactly how Gerald felt, and why. But she was feeling relaxed, so did not want a confrontation with someone who she knew might look twenty, was definitely a lot older, but still viewed the world through childish eyes. She was happy for that to happen at another time, if it had to happen at all.

The more distance Gerald put between himself and the group the more he convinced himself that, through no fault of his own, he had once again arrived in a situation he wanted no part in. Yes, he had made a mistake the night he had come back to the village, but if he had stuck to his original plan, he would have left the town the following morning before the stupid old man had time to cast his nasty little spell. He didn't care what Darl thought, in his mind it had to be the old man who had summoned that dreamwalker. Stuff what Darl had said about the differences between demons and dreamwalkers; it seemed pretty damned demonic to him.

80

He began to wonder just what his future really held. Of course, he thought, the real problem wasn't that people wanted to kill him, but that he wasn't dead. He should have been dead by now, even without the help of the old man's father or the dreamwalker. He was a human who was almost a hundred years old. Humans didn't become almost a hundred years old, almost seventy maybe, never almost a hundred. Immortality, which he had decided he had contracted (for want of a better word), was clearly a curse, and he wanted no part of it. Particularly if his future consisted of being shuffled around between different groups of people who thought he was a liability.

About halfway around the lake, swearing and muttering to himself, full of frustration, he picked up a rock in his left hand and launched it at the water. The rock happened to be a nicely smoothed, flat stone and as it hit the water it skipped once, twice, three times. Gerald watched amazed as it continued jumping four, five, six, seven times before it finally gave into physics and sank beneath the water.

He stood watching the spot where the stone had disappeared. A slight breeze stirred. Branches swayed, and a large swathe of reeds to his right bent towards him. Somewhere in the air he swore he could hear his mother's voice calling him to sit, so he squatted down, and his eyes naturally fell on the water in front of him where he saw his reflection staring back at him. The breeze picked up a little, sending ripples across the lake, shaking his reflection, and seemingly reconfiguring it so that now his mum stared back at him. She smiled, and Gerald rubbed at his eyes unable to believe what he saw.

"Mum?" He whispered at the water. "Is that you?"

"Looking at a reflection is the easiest way to see yourself," his mum replied with a smile. This time he heard the voice loud and clear, as though she was talking directly into his ear.

"What's that meant to mean?" Gerald asked, confused by his mum's words.

"Sometimes things are just what they seem, my love, but it should never stop you from doing the right thing. All things change with time," the reflection replied before the little ripples broke it apart and created a flurry of movement where, for a second, Gerald could have sworn he saw Darl, as a nymph, or perhaps a nymph that looked very similar to her, in the water. He blinked.

The water settled and the breeze disappeared, returning his own face to the mirror surface of the lake. He thought about what his mum had said and continued to stare into his reflection, hoping that a better explained truth or revelation would be forthcoming, but there was nothing. The longer he sat there staring into his own eyes, the less he thought about himself, and the more he thought about Darl. He picked apart the thoughts that had pushed him to walk away from the group. He turned over in his mind everything he had learnt and been exposed to in the past two days. It had been a lot.

Confounded, he lowered his head and closed his eyes. He spoke the prayers of the Guardians out loud. He did his best to visualise each word flying from his mouth, travelling out and around the forest as his mum had always told him to do. The words came easily to him. He had spoken those prayers so many times before, but this was the first time he did so earnestly, immersing himself in them to the total exclusion of the world around him. He spoke praise to the Guardians with a blossoming belief that he found had come quite unexpectedly to him, coursing through his veins, making his heart beat quickly and sending a tingling sensation across his skin. Somewhere in the dark he caught another glimpse of his mum. She was smiling.

He grinned a wide grin as he made his way leisurely back to the camp. He had walked around the lake a million times over the years, seeing far less in all those journeys intended to fill the time between waking and sleeping than he saw in that final stroll. He hadn't changed his mind about his place within the group, or even the world in general. However, he had stumbled, he felt for the first time, on what looked like the green shoots of a new life - an actual, proper life. Isolation had clearly not worked for him, and the coming days, maybe even weeks, were likely to be a bit of a challenge. Yet, he was starting to actually believe that if he could survive, then maybe he had a chance at a future he might want.

As his little hut came into view, he caught the scent of meat roasting. Moments later he heard the sound of Darl and Joggle laughing. Finally, he saw his three companions relaxing on the shore, in almost the same positions as he had left them. Chag watched him approach and Darl broke off her conversation with Joggle to shout to him.

"Perfect timing," she said. "Do you want a glass of ale?"

"No thank you. If there's one thing I've learnt over the past couple of days, it's that me and alcohol really don't belong in the same body," he replied with a smile, as he got closer.

"You seem much happier," Darl said.

"Yeah. That's for sure. Sorry I just went off, but I've had a lot to get my head around the past couple of days," he replied earnestly. "Thank you, by the way. I know I've said it before, but there's a lot to thank you for."

Darl reached out and gave him a hug. It came as something of a shock, and he awkwardly tried to return the gesture, but was unsure how to embrace someone who seemed practically spectral in appearance. He was surprised to find that her body felt firm to his touch. Her glow warmed him, and where the exposed skin of his hands, forearms and face made contact with her, there was that odd tingle that he had felt as he had prayed that afternoon.

The little party ate well and reconvened their discussions once the meal was complete. Gerald quickly realised that the conversations about Joggle joining the group had already happened, and it looked as though he was going to have to get used to hearing the little chap's voice a lot more. Later that evening, as they packed their bags and prepared to start their journey to Tanglehaven the next morning, Gerald, in the spirit of his quest for a new life, approached the irk and asked if he would teach him to count.

"Of course," Joggle gushed. "I would be only too happy to help you in this most important of endeavours. I do wish I had known sooner; maybe the last few years might not have been such a waste."

Gerald thanked the little creature, although he frowned at the dig about his years of lonely uselessness. He had a feeling, though, it was something else he was just going to have to get used to.

The next morning, they rose with the sun and dressed for the day. Darl once again hid herself in her human shell, although her customary skirt and blouse was replaced with loose green trousers tucked into brown boots that rose to her knees, a yellow shirt and well-worn brown leather jacket. Gerald dressed once again in the clothes Darl and Chag had provided for him at the inn, which were now considerably more comfortable for a couple of days of wear. Chag had also changed. He no longer wore the off-white collarless shirt and brown trousers Gerald had seen him in everyday at the bar. He had donned a padded jacket, over which he wore a short mail shirt. A short sword and buckler hung from his left hip and a pair of axes were stuffed into the back of his belt. The moleman's appearance alarmed Gerald. Despite the bandage on his arm, his return to the sanctuary had given him a false sense of security. Faced with Chag looking like he was expecting to fight for each and every step he took towards Tanglehaven reminded him of the dangers ahead of them, and that there would not be a convenient sanctuary for them to shelter in every couple of days.

Chapter 10

Jade spent the night resting on a thick branch in a large tree. She was surprised when she heard the crack of leaves and the snap of twigs underfoot beneath her the next morning. She had expected them to stay a little longer than a single night in the sanctuary. As a demon she did not really sleep but needed, every so often, to spend time in a trancelike state to refresh herself. Her eyes flicked open, and she watched as the moleman and Gerald made their way between the Guardian trees that marked the entrance to the sanctuary. She was further surprised to see that the barmaid also accompanied them, and that an irk had appeared on Gerald's shoulder.

This turn of events was unhelpful. More people meant more eyes and ears looking and listening for anything untoward. It also meant more fists in a fight and more bodies that could get in the way at an inopportune moment. She already had a feeling that the moleman would be a handful to deal with on his own. More people, in short, meant more problems. Admittedly, Jade didn't think the barmaid and the irk looked as though they would present any real threat to her, but her subconscious nagged at her that this was not a time to be taking anything at face value. Surprises and Gerald seemed to go hand in glove, and she had no intention of blundering into the discovery of another one.

On the upside, the number of people who now accompanied Gerald made it easy for Jade to follow him at a relatively safe distance. The party did their best to travel quietly through the woods, but there was always something to be heard and tracks to be followed that gave away the path they had taken. All this meant that Jade did not have to be able to see them to follow them. This was a situation she quite liked because she was only too aware that if she could see someone then, by the immutable laws of logic, there was a chance that they might see her.

As they made their way through the forest, along the old druid trails that cut deep into its heart, Jade overheard snippets of the group's conversations, and what she heard intrigued her. That was once she had gotten over the ego-bruising reality, which in fairness she had suspected, that she was not the reason for their flight.

What most intrigued her though, was the dynamic of the group. It was markedly different to what she had expected. She had guessed that either Gerald or the moleman would be the party's leader, yet it quickly became apparent that the barmaid was the glue that held the group together, and its de facto chief. She would often defer to the moleman, who seemed respected by everyone, on matters concerning the party's safety, and it was Gerald who appeared to be the tag-a-long.

The dynamic itself raised more questions than the information she gathered through her eavesdropping could answer. It became apparent that they were heading to Tanglehaven, and for the first time, Jade found herself trying to guess the reason why she had been employed to kill Gerald. Faint dots were starting to appear, and she could not stop herself from drawing lines between them, but it was clear there were a lot of dots still missing.

After five days of relatively uneventful marching through thick forests, Jade was beginning to think that she had learnt all she would learn from their conversations, and she was bored. She decided it was time to test the group a little, to see just how strong they were and drive out any nasty surprises she might find when, or maybe if, the time came to confront Gerald. Knowing the party's destination and general direction, she left them and headed off into the forest to find some assistance.

As evening fell, Darl set a fire in the small clearing Chag had decided the group would spend the night in. They had not had a fire on any of the previous nights since leaving the sanctuary in case they attracted unwanted attention. Now they were much deeper into the forest, well away from any roads, away even from the druids' trails, walking along the forgotten paths of the nymphs. As there had been no sign of anyone following them, Darl and Chag had decided the greatest threat to them here came from wild animals, which a fire would help deter, as well as providing them with some warmth and the morale-boosting treat of a hot meal. The mention of wild animals, and in particular dark wolves, was enough to send Joggle scurrying up a tree as soon as dinner had been eaten.

"What exactly are dark wolves?" Gerald asked Chag once the evening meal was finished.

"Well, imagine a wolf. Then imagine a wolf that's a bit bigger and has much darker fur," Chag replied, giving Gerald a look that suggested there really were such things as stupid questions and that people shouldn't ask them, at least not of him.

Gerald suddenly noticed that as Chag had been talking to him the moleman's gaze had shifted. He seemed to be staring past Gerald, out into the forest behind him. Chag started to slowly reach over to where his short sword and buckler lay.

"Don't panic," Chag said calmly. "There's one behind you now."

Gerald felt his pulse race.

"Get behind the fire, lad," the moleman growled at him.

"I thought you said the fire would keep wolves away?" Gerald whispered, panic in his voice, as he turned to see a gigantic black wolf prowling through the trees no more than a few meters away from where he sat. The creature moved silently, teeth bared, yellow eyes reflecting the dancing flames.

"Help!" Chag replied quietly.

Gerald froze in confusion, "But you just told me to get behind the fire."

"No, you idiot, I said the fire would help keep animals away. It's far from a guarantee," Chag responded slowly as he moved carefully forwards towards the wolf. "Get yourself behind the fire."

As Gerald stepped delicately around the fire, Darl gave a short sharp cry of alarm. Gerald looked away from the wolf that Chag was facing down and saw two more of the beasts entering the clearing. One was loping towards Darl whilst the other hung back, almost as though it was weighing up which fight it would prefer to be in, or whether to start its own with Gerald.

"How many dark wolves do you get in a pack?" Gerald heard Darl ask nervously.

"Three or four generally," Chag replied without hesitation.

"Okay," Darl said. "There might be another one wandering about out there. Excellent."

Darl was now on her feet and moving nervously back towards the fire.

Chag glanced around quickly. He saw the other wolves closing in on Darl. "By the angels," he said under his breath. "Better get proceedings underway."

He started to bang his short sword against his buckler, taunting the wolf in front of him. In a blur of teeth and claws the creature leapt at him, but the moleman was faster. The buckler went up, its iron-bound rim connecting with the creature's mouth, shattering its lower jaw. Chag committed completely to the attack, so the force of the blow also flung the wolf's head to one side, exposing its throat to his short sword, which plunged into it. Chag felt the blade puncture the throat and dark red blood spurt from the creature's neck, splattering across his face and armour.

The wolf let out a half-hearted gurgling yelp of pain as it sunk to the ground. The creature's death seemed to spur on the other pack members. The wolf nearest to Darl pressed forward, whilst the other, much to

Gerald's surprise, bounded around the fire, determined to take on the moleman.

Darl raised her arms in front of her face as the beast leapt at her. She felt a sharp pain tearing into her left forearm before falling backwards under the weight of the wolf, narrowly missing the fire. The monster growled as it landed on top of her. She screamed as the creature's jaws locked onto her and a bright blue liquid oozed out from between its fangs.

Now it had a hold of her arm the wolf twisted its head back, attempting to wrench the limb away from its socket. Pain surged from her arm into her body, driving her to the brink of unconsciousness. Just as she thought she was about to pass out the growling stopped, and she heard an awkward grunting whine. She glanced about her and watched in horror as Gerald repeatedly rammed his knife into what had, moments before, been the stomach of the wolf. It was now little more than shreds of flesh, ribbons of guts and a growing pool of blood, the by-products of Gerald's desperate, frenzied attack.

"That's enough, lad," Chag shouted, running around the fire having dealt with the third wolf as efficiently as he had dealt with the first. "It's dead, leave it be. There may be more to worry about out there."

Gerald went on stabbing, his eyes focused someway off into the distance, oblivious to Chag's command. When the dark wolf had leapt at Darl, he had stared in horror, frozen to the spot. At some point, which he could not clearly remember, an unfamiliar feeling had crept over him. It had made him draw his knife. It had made him rush to Darl's aid. The next few seconds were hazy, although it could have been minutes or even hours. He felt something on his shoulder, there was a jolt and suddenly he was on his back, knife in the dirt with Chag staring down at him.

"It's over, lad," Chag said.

Gerald found himself back in the reality of the moment. He raised his head and surveyed the remains of the wolf but couldn't quite believe that he had wielded the blade that had created such a mess. His head dropped back, and he closed his eyes. His mind was racing, and his heart was slamming against his chest. He began to take long, deep breaths to calm himself down.

When he finally stood to survey the campsite, the scene shocked him. The three large wolves lay in great pools of blood that had darkened the ground around them. Darl sat with her back to a tree caked in filth, torn lengths of cloth wrapped around her left forearm. The irk stood close to her with what was, for him, a large bowl of filthy water.

"Darl, are you alright?" he asked, running the couple of steps to her side.

"Thanks to you, I'm alive," she replied through gritted teeth.

"I wish I'd had a bit more of clue as to what I actually did. It's all a bit of a blur now," he replied in a wavering voice.

"Doesn't matter. You did something, although next time it wouldn't hurt for you to be quicker about it," Chag said, coming up behind them.

"Don't crowd her," Joggle piped up, now grinding herbs together in another bowl and waving a paw to shoo them away. "She needs some space, and I am more than capable of dressing her wounds on my own. Your time would be much better spent getting rid of those brutes."

Gerald stared blankly at the dark wolf carcasses that the irk was talking about. "What are we meant to do with them then? Can we eat them?" he asked, as it dawned on him just how big the creatures were and how difficult it would be to get rid of them, at least in one piece.

"You can, but if you do, I won't be having any. Not while there's fresh soil to be eaten and enjoyed far more," Chag replied, fishing a pipe and some tobacco out of one of the many pouches he had about his person.

"Not a delicacy then?" Gerald asked.

"Not anywhere I'd want to spend any time," Chag replied. "And as to what we're going to do with them, the answer is nothing. They can stay and give any other hungry beasties an alternative meal choice to us. We're packing up, and as soon as Darl is able to make a move, we're leaving."

"But she needs plenty of rest," Joggle protested.

"Eventually. It's my arm that's hurt, not my legs. I can still walk. I'll rest when we get to the city. I've only got one good arm left so I'm not waiting around for another encounter like that," Darl said firmly, with a look that made it very clear as to how any further medical advice from the irk would be taken.

Jade watched the proceedings with mixed feelings. The dark wolves had taken quite a bit of effort to track down and cajole towards the camp, so watching the moleman despatch two in a matter of seconds felt somewhat disappointing. She could have thrown a couple of rabbits at them instead, she thought; it would have required far less effort on her part and achieved much the same results. It had, however, confirmed her suspicions that taking him on in a fair fight was probably not something she would be looking to do in the near future. So, if she was going to kill Gerald, it was going to have to be while the moleman wasn't looking, or better still wasn't anywhere within a several-mile radius.

Jade had also been taken back by Gerald's reaction. She'd had him down as the person most likely to run screaming into the forest, but after a brief moment of indecision, he'd waded in dagger drawn and stabbed a wolf to death. Admittedly, the wolf had been pre-occupied with the barmaid's arm, but it still looked like he might be developing a spine, which she considered decidedly unhelpful in a potential target.

Mostly though, she had to admit that the spark of a feeling somewhere between interest and admiration, that had ignited within her for the little group of reprobates, was growing. Heroes they certainly weren't, but they seemed capable of getting things done. That was a good thing in Jade's view. She liked people who could get things done far more than heroes, or villains for that matter. It made her all the more interested to find out what they were up to.

With the wolves dead and Darl's arm bandaged, Gerald volunteered to take the first watch. Chag was only too happy to oblige, and it wasn't long until the moleman was gently snoring.

"How does he do that?" Gerald asked Darl, who was still awake.

"Practice, I guess. I don't think you can be too choosy about where you sleep when you're out soldiering, and he certainly soldiered for a good few years," Darl replied still propped up against the tree. She carefully got up using her right hand and walked slowly over to where Gerald sat staring out into the dark between the trees.

"Careful," Gerald said, seeing her wince in pain. "Didn't Joggle tell you to stay seated?"

"It's alright. I'm alright. You should know by now I'm not like other girls," she laughed. "This won't take long to heal."

Gerald looked concerned but was not going to argue with the nymph. "What about you?" she asked. "How's your hand?"

"I am like other boys. Kind of. It's on the mend," he said. Then, as an unwanted flash of memory reminded him that he had stabbed the wolf with his blade in his left hand, added, "Fortunately, I've always been as good with my left as I have with my right."

"That's lucky," Darl replied, with a smile and a sideways glance that Gerald wasn't quite sure how to interpret.

"Thanks, by the way. I think I owe you one now," Darl said.

"Not so sure about that. I reckon we're probably about even, for the time being," Gerald replied.

"Well, I mean unless you count the rose," Darl said with a wink.

90

"Well, I mean… yeah, other than the rose," Gerald stuttered, suddenly feeling very deflated.

Nestled in her tree, Jade listened to Gerald and Darl's conversation as they passed their time on watch. Ordinarily she made a point of not listening into the conversations of people she had been employed to remove from existence. It wasn't so much that she didn't have an interest in what people had to say; it was more because she considered the resulting accumulation of knowledge quite dangerous. Over the years she had found that knowledge seemed to be quite a common cause of death. Technically, of course, she was the actual cause of death, but that was not how she saw it. Jade simply did not consider herself to be a killer, at least not the wanton murdering type. After all, she never woke up wanting to kill people. Other people woke up wanting to kill people; she simply offered a service that fulfilled those people's needs. She considered herself to be more of a tool. She would grudgingly stretch to being considered a weapon, but then that was really only a very specific type of tool. The way she saw it was that no sword had ever actually cut someone's head off without a person picking it up and waving it around first. The same logic could be applied to wooden spoons, spatulas and the brushes used to clean toilets, and no one was calling them weapons. Replace "sword" with "Jade" and "picking it up and waving it around" with "paying" and there it was, incontrovertible proof that she was a tool.

The amount of knowledge someone had was also important when it came to determining how terminal knowing stuff was. Jade had generally noticed that people who had no knowledge of anything very rarely upset anyone to the point that someone would pay good money to have them killed. She felt she was a case in point. In all the centuries she had provided her services to those in need of them, and with sufficient capital to pay for them, she had never once been interested in anything other than what she was being paid for, and, as far as she was aware, no one had ever tried to kill her because of it.

On the other hand, the people who hired her tended to be the ones who had all the knowledge. She knew this because sometimes they wanted her to know it. That invariably meant that she would have to sit through tedious monologues full of bluster and bravado, which she tolerated only because they were paying for her time and attention. So, it seemed all too often she ended up hunting down the people in the middle. The people who knew too much about something for them to be allowed to live but didn't know enough to make them worth keeping alive. Listening into conversations, Jade believed, was the first step on the slippery slope to taking an interest, which meant you then ran the risk of getting a little insight. This could result in you forming an opinion, and if you weren't careful forming an opinion could lead to you taking a side; which could be particularly problematic if the side you took wasn't the side you were being paid to be on. A little knowledge could, without a doubt, lead to very dangerous places.

Jade had, from an early age, reasoned that in order to become someone who knew everything, you first had to move through that dangerous middle stage of being a person who knew something, and that was a risk she didn't want to take. She knew no one would ever mistake her for a genius, but she was damned if she was going to get caught out doing something as stupid as trying to be clever. In this case, however, she was finding it increasingly difficult to not make an exception. She wondered if it was the boredom setting in again.

The conversation didn't exactly flow between Gerald and Darl, but it was clear that was because the thing they were talking about, that they referred to occasionally as the rose, was also something they were both trying to avoid discussing. Clearly this rose, whatever it was code for, was the reason for their journey. Another dot of information was added to Jade's growing collection, and suddenly she found herself wanting to know what Gerald had been doing in Tanglehaven all those years ago, and why he was going back? Jade was now on the slippery slope.

Eventually, Gerald and the barmaid's watch came to an end and the moleman took over. The conversation ended and, with the moleman standing watch alone, Jade knew no further titbits of information would be forthcoming. She settled into a comfortable position and meditated until the morning came.

The next day brought a further change to the group's dynamics. Not surprisingly the attack had put them on edge. The moleman took charge now. Before they had been wanderers; now they were soldiers. They moved in complete silence, as quickly as they could. There were no more fires or friendly conversations. The only actions they took were those essential to a safe and speedy arrival at their destination.

Chapter 11

Three days after the wolf attack, the party arrived outside Tanglehaven at about noon. They were exhausted from an increase in pace and a reduction in sleep that Chag had pushed them to achieve, that they might get out of the wild as quickly as possible.

They stood on the edge of the forest looking up at the towering city walls that stood just a few hundred metres away. Gerald remembered very little of the city itself, but its great grey stone walls punctuated by tall towers, with flags and banners fluttering in the breeze like the castles in the tales of his mum, were emblazoned upon his memory. The city was a world away from the ragged assortment of hovels that had once made-up Spindle. The forest stopped abruptly, and long grass grew all the way from the treeline to the base of the hill on which the city had been built. Tree stumps of varying ages were hidden amongst the grass, some cut recently, others little more than mounds of damp wood covered in red and yellow mushrooms.

A wide dirt road ran in front of the spot between the trees they emerged from. It ran from east to west, and not far from where they stood, it split into two. One road continued straight on, eventually disappearing into the forest that surrounded the city, except where land gave way to the ocean in the east. The second bent sharply back in on itself before climbing the steep hill to a gatehouse, and the city beyond.

They joined the road and followed it up the hill. Despite a sharp incline, the comparatively flat surface made the last steps of their journey far easier going than the uneven, branch-strewn forest floor had. As they got about halfway up the hill, they noticed a small track running to their left that disappeared around the side of the city walls. Tired, ragged people trudged along the track and joined the main road before heading into the city, whilst others made the journey from the city to the track before disappearing out of sight around the wall. His interest piqued, Joggle dropped down from Gerald's shoulder and ran alongside the dirt track to see where it led. Gerald followed, concerned that the irk might get lost, or trodden on.

Hidden from the view of the main path was a shanty town propped up against the mighty city wall. It looked so insignificant standing against the great edifice that loomed over it. Gerald instantly recognised in the people who walked the thin, muddy path the desperation that he had seen in

Tanglehaven. Something about staring it in the face once again made him feel uncomfortable, and he called to Joggle to return to the group with him. Joggle sat in the grass, back straight, head twitching, taking in the scenes of makeshift houses built from the rubbish the city had thrown away and the people who made it their home. There was an irony, he thought, that the more he learnt about humans, the less he understood them. When he had first discovered them, he had been impressed by their capacity to thrive almost anywhere, because of their ability to work together and live in communities. But the more he watched them, the more he began to see that although humans gravitated to one another to create those communities, each individual was in constant competition with every other individual for the same finite resources. Surely, he wondered, given that these creatures were capable of such hugely complex creations as Tanglehaven, providing a comfortable home and food for everyone who contributed to the community should not have been beyond them. And yet this never seemed a priority for those humans who controlled the greatest amounts of wealth. Humans, he had decided a long time ago, were a deeper mystery than the immortals. Gerald's calls snapped him out of his thoughts. He took one last look at the awkward dwellings on the side of the hill before scampered back to the main road.

The massive gates to the city were open, and there was no guard to stop them walking in, or ask who they were, or where they were from. They looked up as they passed through the gatehouse to see the dark openings in the ceiling, where the points of portcullises could just about be made out. Chag breathed a sigh of relief as they walked under the massive arches of the tunnel into the city. Having spent so long in Spindle-Upon-Spindle, he had forgotten the city would sometimes close itself off to outsiders if it felt threatened. He should have known to take this into consideration when planning the journey, but the thought had not even crossed his mind until now. He thanked the gods for the easy entry, before berating himself for not remembering to even consider it. It may not have turned out to be important this time, but surprises could cost lives and it was not a mistake he would have made in his younger years. It made him feel old.

To Gerald the gates may as well have been a portal between two different planes of existence, such was the contrast between the quiet countryside outside the city walls and the riot of sound and colour within. He could not remember the place being so busy, or the intensity of the pitch and heave of humanity as the city went about its daily life.

Chag led the way through what started out as a confusion of people, all bustling, hustling, shouting, and waving, that slowly rationalised itself into a market square. Like Spindle-Upon-Spindle, the market square comprised temporary stalls made of wood and cloth, and traders with barrows in the middle, whilst around the outside there were neat little rows of shops and inns that marked out the trading space. Unlike Spindle-Upon-Spindle, though, this market square was massive. Standing at the edge, Gerald wondered how anyone found anything they needed, the place was a bedazzlement of colours, sweet smells and competing voices yelling in any number of different languages. Joggle felt a little overwhelmed and wondered, given the size of the square and the sheer volume of people crammed into it, how long it would take him to cross from one side to the other. In the end he gave up and decided that journey, if it ever had to be made, would be made on Gerald's shoulder.

They walked around the edge of the square, where there was just about enough space for the party to move together, staying at least within sight of each other. They went from inn to inn looking for a place to stay, but most had signs in their windows to show they were full. Chag eventually slipped into the first building he saw that looked clean and well-kept and had a "rooms available" sign on the door. He raised an eyebrow as the innkeeper told him the cost of a room. He wondered if that was why the inn seemed to be one of the few presentable looking ones that still had beds available for the night.

The bar on the ground floor was full of merchants and travellers which, despite the cost, made Chag feel comfortable about the choice of lodgings. He hoped that a clientele made up of those who were, by and large, unknown to the wider city as much as they were to each other would be one in which they were less likely to stand out.

When they opened the door to their room, the moleman had to grudgingly admit that maybe, just maybe, the place wasn't as much of a rip-off as he had initially judged it to be. Even for three people and Joggle, the room was generously proportioned. In the centre of the room was a massive four poster bed made of highly polished, dark wood with two richly embroidered yellow curtains on each side. The curtains had been drawn back to the corner posts and tied with short, thick golden rope, revealing crisp white sheets pulled tight over the mattress. A pair of white pillows were propped up against a headboard that had figures, with animal heads and fish bodies, enjoying a feast carved into it.

A large chaise longue with a blue velvet covering and matching cushions had been placed at the foot of the bed, and a pair of large trunks crafted in the same wood as the bed stood on either side of it. Gerald breathed a sigh of relief. He had worried that the events of the last few days had set a tone for the rest of the adventure. A suspicion had even sneaked over him, as they climbed the last half of the hill to the city gate, that Chag or Darl would suggest staying in the shanty town to avoid detection, so the sight that met his weary eyes was a welcome one.

As soon as the door was closed behind them, Darl dropped the small shoulder bag she had been carrying and made a beeline for the chaise longue. She plumped the already plump cushions before lying down and stretching out.

"Watch your dirty clothes on that thing," Chag scolded. "I'm only paying to sleep here, not to redecorate once we've left."

Darl stuck her tongue out at Chag. She stood, walked to the bed and yanked one of the sheets off. She draped it loosely around herself and wriggled out of her dirty clothes.

"Is that better?" she asked Chag with a cheeky smile.

"Just make sure the furniture stays clean," Chag replied, shaking his head and rolling his eyes, as Darl made her way back to the chaise longue.

"Now I'm no longer a threat to the upholstery, I believe you two have some business to attend to," she said, extending her good arm and waving towards the door. "After all, I'm far too injured to do anything but rest. Joggle's orders."

Gerald's heart sank. When he'd agreed to Chag and Darl's little scheme, he hadn't expected to be walking away from such a luxurious room. At this point, though, he was so tired he would have felt pretty much the same about any waterproof building with a flat surface large enough for him to lie down on.

"Come on lad," Chag said. Gerald noticed that during his brief exchange with Darl the moleman had found a long, dark green, woollen coat from somewhere. He had thrown it over his travelling clothes, including the chainmail, presumably to hide the various weapons stuffed into his belt. Gerald smiled, because whilst it did the job it was required to do very well, Chag now looked as though he had put on quite a bit of weight over the last couple of weeks. There was something quite comical about his thin, molelike face, which now seemed to be perched upon a four-and-a-half-foot tall green barrel with feet.

If Chag noticed Gerald's now stifled smile, he didn't say anything and headed straight for the door. "You relax," he called to Darl. "And remember you're meant to be in great pain."

"Send someone up to draw me a bath, darling, please," Darl shouted after him. Chag rolled his eyes again and pulled the door shut.

They left the room, which was on the first floor, and made their way through tiny, sparsely decorated corridors. Gerald was anxious, and with each step he took towards the ground floor of the inn, and its public bar, his nerves nibbled away at him.

After the wolf attack Darl had become convinced that someone, or something, was following them. At first Chag had been dismissive, but mile after mile Darl's concerns grew. Gerald overheard her whispered conversations with Chag, in which she referred to whatever it was she felt as a malign influence. Immediately following the attack Gerald hadn't noticed anything either, but the next morning he started to feel an occasional shiver come over him. He heard the odd snap of a twig that seemed to come from deep in the forest where he thought no one should have been, and then there was the occasional leaf that didn't seem to fall in quite the right way, although he wouldn't have been able to explain what the right way should have been. Chag dismissed Gerald's observations as the movement of animals, which, he reminded Gerald quite sarcastically, were generally to be found in the forests. Unsurprisingly, Chag's sarcasm did nothing to allay Gerald's suspicions, that turned rapidly to fear as he felt a familiar sensation - the sensation of a cold claw reaching out for him. He inserted himself into Darl's and Chag's whispered conversations, supporting Darl's concerns.

Chag, who was not one to believe something simply because everyone else did, especially when there was no real evidence to support their suspicions, generally trusted Darl's instincts. So, as the second day drew to a close, seeing Darl was still concerned, he agreed it would not hurt to see if they could spot anyone who might be on their trail. They agreed that the forest was so dense it would be far too easy for anyone following them to evade any attempts they made to find them. Instead, they decided to wait until they reached the city to see if Darl and Gerald were right, and a plan was devised.

The plan was not complex. Concerns about being spied upon limited the extent to which the party could talk freely about their fears, and how they might turn the tables on whoever it was they believed was following them. It was also not a very good plan, and whilst no one said it out loud, each member of the party knew it had a lot of limitations and relied heavily on a lot of assumptions. This awareness made each of them, in their own way, focus more on what their adventure was really about and why they were there. They each asked themselves if they really believed in what they were doing, if they believed they could do what they had set out to do, but no one shared their answers to the questions that they each hoped no one else was dwelling on.

The wolf attack had brought into sharp focus the rush with which they'd entered into the hunt for the rose and exposed, not only the gaps in the plans Darl and Chag had laid, but the weakness of the foundations that underpinned the expedition. They individually came to the realisation that they were constantly reacting, without proper thought, to threats and attacks they did not really understand the reasons for or know who was behind. So, whilst the plan was bad, each of them saw in it a fine thread of opportunity that they so desperately wanted to grab at. An opportunity to find out who was after them and give them a chance to take hold of some sort of control.

As they entered the bar Chag stopped and looked around. Gerald's nerves had gotten the better of him. He focused only on Chag and his instructions, to the exclusion of everything else that was going on around him.

"Okay, lad, let's have a quick drink and then we can go and grab your stuff," Chag said. Gerald noticed that Chag's delivery was quite forced, as though he had been preparing the line for some time, and his voice was far louder than usual.

Chag was many things, but he was no actor. Pretence created complexities that could betray a person, he had always thought, better to wear your colours with pride. It was why as a soldier he had ended up becoming a mercenary. He saw an honest consistency in choosing to fight for a day's wages. Better that than fighting for an ideal that could change as suddenly as the direction of a flag in the wind.

It was Chag's straightforward and honest nature that had endeared him to Darl when they had first met. It had made their business partnership so effortless and enduring, just like the friendship that had blossomed out of it. His honesty meant he was far from suited to subterfuge. So, as he spoke just a bit too loudly and ushered them towards a table in the middle of the bar, so they could be plainly seen to be having a quick drink before going to pick up "Gerald's stuff", Gerald found himself snapping out of his nervous state to confidently challenge the moleman's suggestion.

"Not there," Gerald whispered as Chag was about to sit down. "It's too obvious."

Both Chag and Gerald were as equally shocked by Gerald's pronouncement. Gerald had heard the words in his head, only realising he had said them out loud as he noticed the moleman's grimace at his challenge to him. Instinctively knowing that the lad was right, and not wanting to cause a scene, Chag let Gerald take the lead. Gerald led them to a small table in a quiet corner of the bar. The table was partially obscured from view by a statue, that looked so out of place that Gerald wondered if someone had bought it in the market, popped in for a quick drink, and forgotten to take it home.

"Why here?" asked Chag irritably as they took their seats.

"You work in an inn. When was the last time you saw a couple of dodgy types sat in the middle of the bar, broadcasting their plans in the hope that everyone can hear? If there is someone following us, and they're here watching us now, we need to make this look at least halfway realistic," Gerald said, sounding so confident he surprised himself.

Jade's ears prickled as soon as she heard the moleman's voice. In her human form, with her oversized bag and heavy stick resting on the floor at her feet, she sat facing away from the bar in a large armchair angled towards a roaring log fire. A small glass of sherry nestled between her fingers, which were interlaced in a manner that Jade felt was the proper way for old people to hold small glasses of sherry. Keen that Gerald and the moleman should not leave without her in tow, she downed the drink and tottered over to the bar, stick in hand, pretending to be in search of a refill. As she tottered, she scanned the tables and standing areas for a glimpse of the pair.

"Strange," Chag said, catching sight of the old lady before she was able to see them.

"What?" Gerald asked.

"I recognise that old lady at the bar from somewhere, but I can't place her," Chag said.

Gerald carefully twisted in his seat to catch a glimpse of the old woman. "Can't say I've ever clapped eyes on her before, but I'd certainly recognise that stick of hers anywhere."

It didn't take long for Gerald and Chag to work out where they recognised the woman, and the stick, from.

"Odd," Chag said pensively. "You don't think this could be anything other than a coincidence?"

"Appearances can be deceiving," Gerald replied, an image of Darl in the sheet drifting into his mind. "The old man did sort of imply he was going to send a demon after me. Maybe she's the demon, and the stick is some sort of talisman to control her or communicate with her?"

Chag laughed quietly, "Control a demon? You humans crack me up. Nothing can control a demon. If he was stupid enough to call on one for help, it's much more likely she took a fancy to the stick and killed him for it. Still, at least we have a suspect. Shall we get this over with?"

Gerald gave a nod, nerves returning. They stood up. Gerald casually knocked his mug over, and loudly pretended it was an accident for good measure, before heading for the door.

Jade watched them leave, then ran back to her chair, no longer bothering with her old lady walk. She grabbed the oversized bag and threw the strap over her shoulder. It did cross her mind that she might be hurrying into a trap, but by the time she made it into the street Gerald and Chag were disappearing around a corner a few metres away. They were moving at quite a pace, which convinced her that whilst they might have been concerned about being followed, they were certainly not waiting around for anyone to catch them up.

As they turned the corner and disappeared out of sight, she allowed herself another little run and a gentle barge of someone who was in her way. As she reached the turning, she unbuttoned her jacket, more a cardigan, and rested her hand on the pommel of a pistol stowed within one of the many hidden pockets she sewed into all her clothes. She slowed down and, drawing a deep breath, turned the corner prepared to draw the pistol and shoot at the slightest hint of the moleman or the lad waiting for her. Nothing - well, not nothing, but there was no sight of Gerald or the moleman waiting for her with a big hammer at least.

There were people moving around the streets. They were doing whatever it was people did when they weren't sleeping, working, or eating, but crucially there was no ambush. She looked further down the street just in time to see Gerald turn another corner. She ran, as best she could, through the crowd to catch up with them. The next street they turned into was busy. It looked like another main shopping street. It was wide, but the volume of people made it hard to navigate because of the way they milled around. This wasn't one of those streets that connected two places which people shuffled between. The busy shopfronts built up either side, and the barrows in the middle, meant people were constantly moving in every direction. Jade did her best to dodge and weave through them, but her human form was not exactly built for agility. To make matters worse her shoulder bag was awkward and seemed to catch on pretty much everyone and everything that passed her on the side she was carrying it, including a young pickpocket's hand. The young man was lucky Jade's attention was elsewhere; under normal circumstances she would have made time to demonstrate to the boy why you don't steal from demons, before demonstrating why he would never be able to steal from anyone else ever again. Instead, by the time she realised his little hand was rooting around in her bag, her only recourse was to mutter the words of one of the few spells she knew that would turn the boy's fingers into live herrings for three days.

She focused on Gerald, because by now Chag had disappeared from sight. She knew she should have kept an eye on both of them, but they were moving too fast. Not only that, but the moleman was considerably shorter than the majority of other people in the street so was far harder to keep track of, even more so because she did not exactly tower over the other pedestrians. Anyway, she reasoned, Gerald was the one to keep her eye on. From what she had heard it was something of his, hidden when he had last been in the city, that the party had set out to retrieve.

The journey went on and on. She wondered once or twice if Gerald was lost, but he walked with such confidence she dismissed the notion. Then, as the streets started to get smaller and people became more occasional and shops turned into houses, she suddenly realised the moleman had disappeared. Instinctively she grabbed at the pistol in her cardigan as she felt a sharp point applying pressure on the back of her thigh.

"What's the matter? Can't reach my back?" Jade muttered.

"Slow down, but keep walking," Chag said quietly. "And don't think about trying any funny business. How long have you been following us for?"

"How long have you known I've been following you?" she countered coldly.

"This really isn't the way this works," Chag said in a tone that Jade knew only too well. "Pretty sure we're in the part of town where people don't ask questions and are quick to forget the things they know they're not meant to see. Want to test that theory out?"

"Yes. let's," Jade muttered, slowly pulling the pistol from her pocket.

She felt something slam into the back of her knees. She was lifted off the ground and dropped onto the cobbles. It was a hard landing and her back bore the brunt of it. She lay on the street trying to catch her breath. Being immortal, she generally didn't worry too much about being killed in circumstances like this; however, immortality doesn't protect you from being tied up and dragged off to somewhere dark and out of the way. So rather than waiting for someone to jump on her, or put a bag over her head, she pointed the pistol up into the sky and pulled the trigger.

The moleman was right about the area. Screaming help in that lonely alley, in that run-down part of the city, only made people remember all the reasons they needed to be anywhere else but there at that precise moment. It would get roughly the same response as knocking an old lady to the street with practised skill and the obvious intent to do something that was unlikely to be very nice to her. So, she didn't bother trying to scream. However, Jade knew full well that if you set fire to something or blew something up in an area like this, for some reason, people would crawl over one another to find out what was going on.

The sound of the shot shattered the silence. The shuttered windows on either side of the alley suddenly opened; so too did doors that looked like they hadn't been used in decades, and people rushed out. A surprising number of people who had been loitering in other lonely alleys started to appear from around corners. Within seconds of the shot being fired the alley was full of people and, as Chag looked around trying to gauge the likely outcome of this unexpected turn of events, Jade took the opportunity to roll away and disappear into the crowd.

She fled through more lonely alleys, turning into different streets at every opportunity, occasionally looking back to see if Gerald or the moleman were following her. For the first time in a long time, she had become the hunted. The boot was on the other foot, and it felt incredibly uncomfortable. She had no idea where she was heading, but right now all she wanted to do was put distance between them and her. After dodging around five or six corners, she noticed the buildings that composed those corners had changed. The run-down backstreets that served as homes to the city's poor had become the factories and warehouses where they worked. She slowed her pace to a walk, listening for any sounds that might give away a pursuer.

As she walked, she surveyed the massive buildings for signs of disuse and abandonment, not only by merchants, but also by the homeless and destitute. She eventually found an old warehouse with heavy locks on the doors, boarded-up windows, and the distinct look of inactivity. She checked behind her once again before pulling the mace from her bag. With one smooth movement she raised it above her head and brought it down hard on a large padlock that held two thick bands of metal together. The chunky body of the lock fell away. She pulled the remaining loop of metal out from the holes it sat in, that had been drilled through the metal bands. The bands were hinged either side of the door, and the hinges had been screwed into the wooden doorframe. Without the padlock to hold them in place they swung open, and Jade made her way inside.

Unsurprisingly, it was dark, which wasn't an issue for a creature of the eternal Abyss. She walked through the large empty rooms, noting a lingering smell of grain and alcohol. It was a single-storey building, so there was only the ground floor to investigate and as everything appeared to have been removed, it did not take long for her to find the only locked door that did not lead back outside. She forced the door and found it led to what she assumed had been the office of whoever ran the little business. It was the one room that still had any furniture in it. The furniture was basic and nothing to get excited about, but more than sufficient for her purposes. There was a chair and a table close to the door. The table had a few scraps of paper on it that had yellowed with age and been chewed by mice.

She sat at the table and picked up a sheet of paper. She turned it around in her hands in a fidgety manner, first from one side to the other a few times, before laying it flat on the table and rotating it. She folded it several times before tearing small pieces from it, in an attempt to distract herself from the questions swimming about in her head. But it was no good, they demanded answers. What was Gerald here to get? Was she still following him, or was he now following her? Why hadn't she killed him yet?

It took her a while to settle on any kind of answer, let alone find the right words to express it. Even then she wasn't happy with what finally popped out of her mouth, addressed to no one else but her and the empty dark of the building.

"It's messy," she said. "I don't like messy."

Jade had never been a fan of grey areas, or situations where she had to rely on her initiative. She liked things to be simple, or more precisely, clear. She liked being an order taker, a cog in a machine. It made her life easy. For all the megalomaniacs, tyrants, and villains she'd worked for over the years she had never thought, not even once, that she wanted to be one. That way, she had seen all too often, madness lay, and she wasn't interested in visiting. But for all the madness she had seen over the years, there had been thought put into it. There were detailed plans and schemes. She might have been trusted to do her job in her own way, but her employers still wanted to know when it had been completed. They wanted evidence, which was fair enough. But most importantly of all, they knew absolutely everything there was to know about whoever it was that she was being paid to visit.

The voice that had employed her had a plan, at least it had said it had a plan. Yet it hadn't known that Gerald was immortal. That was a big thing to not know about someone who was supposedly so important to you that they needed killing.

It was even more important information for her. Not knowing that had meant she had shown up to kill Gerald with the wrong tools, which had meant she had improvised. The plan had been sound: in her mind. She had killed everyone else in the same room as Gerald and chopped them up into tiny pieces, so that when they were discovered in the morning, Gerald would be arrested, which would make him easy to find. She could then return a bit later with the right tools and finish the job she had been paid to do. Of course, it hadn't worked out like that. Gerald had woken up before her butchery could be discovered, slipped out the window and run home. And that was the next big thing her employer had failed to tell her. Not only was he immortal, but he lived in a bloody sanctuary.

Even more frustrating, now more than ever, was the subsequent disappearance of her employer. She had only spoken to the voice once when it had arranged the contract with her. A little while after their conversation she was paid, before the job had been completed, which was unheard of. After that, she had heard nothing, not even a request to see some sort of evidence to confirm that the job had been done.

Jade wanted to see her employer's disappearance as a positive, but it was not. It only added to the mess. She sighed deeply. She wanted to walk away, but she couldn't. She'd learnt that the hard way a long time ago. As frustrated and irritated as she was, there were too many loose ends that could come back to bite her one day. No, she had to sort out the mess this time. It didn't mean having to kill Gerald, which was becoming far less appealing now the moleman was involved and they knew that she was on their trail, but it did mean being certain of what it might mean for her if she didn't.

She tore a final tiny piece from the tightly folded paper in her hand before slowly unfolding it and holding it up in triumph, displaying a tiny chain of five paper skulls to the universe for its approval. She smiled. She wasn't usually one for puzzles, but there was something so spectacularly odd about the whole situation she now found herself in, that even she could not help but be intrigued.

Chapter 12

After the pistol shot had shaken the backstreets and alleys into life, Chag and Gerald ran. They headed in the direction that offered the least resistance, and as they had been at opposite ends of the alley that meant they ran in opposite directions. Gerald ran blindly down the first alley he saw that led away from the incident. Meanwhile, Chag, who had something of a knack for finding his way around places, bolted back in the direction he had come from, heading straight for the inn. Gerald, on the other hand, took a lot longer to find his bearings. That was partly because he did not have the moleman's natural sense of direction, partly because he had run off into parts of the city he had not already walked through, and partly because he was too scared to ask anyone for any help. Eventually, though, he stopped running and tried to work out where he was.

Being alone for the first time in a few days felt strangely invigorating. Even though he was getting used to his companions, having them around constantly over the last couple of weeks had made him feel a little claustrophobic. He enjoyed Darl's company, Chag was generally bearable, and then there was Joggle. Joggle was Joggle, and whilst he was growing fond of the little creature, Chag's not overly polite request that Joggle shut up for the remainder of the journey following the wolf attack had been welcomed by everyone. Gerald briefly wondered how Darl would be coping alone with the irk. Joggle, he decided, would undoubtedly be making up for lost talking time. He didn't envy her at that particular moment.

He had run as fast as he could away from the chaos that had ensued after the old woman had fired what he guessed was a gun of some sort. What a noise it had made. He had heard stories of the mysterious black powder that could be used to make tiny weapons more powerful than any bow, but they were very rare, and this was the first time he had actually heard one go off, although he had not properly seen it.

Having caught his breath, he began to walk at a relaxed pace. He felt he was now far enough away from the incident, that he could at least make a plausible attempt at denying he had been anywhere near it if anyone asked. He wasn't worried about Chag. The moleman knew how to look after himself. As for the old lady, or possible demon, or whatever she was, he assumed that she would have caught up to him by now if she had wanted to

106

or had been in a position to do so. So, he found himself feeling as though he might actually be able to have a little time for himself without someone trying to kill him. Although he continued to look around nervously and occasionally doubled back on himself, just in case. The longer he walked for the more his mind calmed, pushing away the near-constant feeling of fear that had dogged him since the dreamwalker had attacked him. As his mind eased, he began to feel the reassuring anonymity of the city folding its arms around him once again, just as he had when he had arrived in Spindle-Upon-Spindle to find that no one wanted to hang him. He smiled and let the energy of the people around him wash over him. It felt good.

He could feel something starting to blossom inside himself, a curiosity. A large man bustled down the street ahead of him dressed in bright, clean clothes trimmed with fur. He was clearly a man of wealth and significant substance, in more than one sense. A bag hung from his shoulder and as Gerald got closer to him, he noticed nestled inside was a pouch that he instinctively seemed to know contained coins.

A moment later Gerald walked leisurely past the man, having fished the pouch from his bag, confirmed that the pouch did indeed contain a number of large golden coins, removed one, and returned the slightly lighter purse to the bag. Gerald smiled at just how easy it still was, and it reminded him a little of his childhood, although he could never remember stealing coins.

Whilst he had always thought of himself as a thief of necessities, the reality was that Spindle had been so impoverished it would have been quite a challenge for him to find anything to steal that wasn't a necessity. No one in Spindle had anything of any real value to be stolen, but even if they had, his life was so simple that twelve-year-old Gerald would not have known what to do with it, and of course his mum would have made him give it back.

Significantly older Gerald, on the other hand, knew exactly what to spend his newly acquired coin on. It wasn't long before he stood, legs apart and arms outstretched, with a tailor measuring him for new clothes. They had travelled light from Spindle-Upon-Spindle, and he felt a change was in order. His only other set of clothes, the clothes he had originally set out from the sanctuary in, were now a small pile of ash in a much bigger pile of ash. The clothes he wore bore the stains of their travels, and their encounter with the wolves. And whilst, in the main, the inhabitants of Tanglehaven where not pristine in their appearance, their worn hemlines adorned by the dust and dirt of the city, they looked positively well-heeled compared to him in his savaged vestiary.

The tailor finished taking his measurements, and offered an additional payment for speed, set about making the new trousers, shirt and jacket, which he promised faithfully would be ready for the following morning. By a stroke of luck, the tailor and Gerald shared similar measurements, so Gerald was also able to secure an immediate change of clothes. This also gave him further reassurance that if the old woman was trying to find him, he would now be a little harder to spot.

Relieving a street trader of an apple, almost without realising that he had done so, Gerald made his way back to the main street that ran through the centre of the walled city. But rather than heading back to the inn, he decided there was ample time for him to enjoy his moment of freedom a little longer. After spending so many years cut off from the world, he felt as though he was undergoing some kind of awakening that he did not want to slow down or stop, which he feared might happen if he returned to the inn too soon.

Being with the company had created mixed feelings in him. Whilst outwardly he was comfortable being around them, inwardly he still felt the same anxieties he had felt by the lake, before he had finally decided to leave his empty hut and set out to make something of his empty life. Being around them as they effortlessly demonstrated the knowledge, experiences, and skills they had each built up over their lifetimes made him feel as though he existed only to be someone to be looked after and coddled. He often found himself feeling as though they treated him like a child, in constant need of direction and supervision. Now, out on his own, he felt at last like he finally had an opportunity to start searching for the him he so desperately wanted to find.

He decided the time had come for him to own his identity, to embrace the role he apparently, according to Darl's stories, had played: the role of the master thief. After all, he had stolen from Death and gotten away with it, so there had to be some truth in it. Didn't there?

Another keen motivator driving his desire to find some kind of identity was the suspected demonic granny, with a penchant for explosions, who was out to get him. Whilst he had, until recently, been wholly indifferent about his own life and death, he felt he was now dabbling in something approaching a normal life. And he was starting to consider that, whilst demons and dreamwalkers were not a reason to get up in the morning, there were plenty of other things that were.

He had been less than convinced when Darl and Chag had outlined their plan to confront Death to him in the inn, but the attack that night had been the spur in his side. Although he had not raised it with Chag in the bar that afternoon, the possibility that the old woman was the demon the angry old man at the door of the Muddy Toad had threatened to send after him, had started him thinking about the dreamwalker once again.

As he made his way through the city streets, his thoughts returned to pondering who else might have sent it, if not the old man. He was beginning to wonder if it had been Death. Death had a motive, after all he had stolen from him. Death also, he assumed, had eyes and ears everywhere. It was not beyond believable that one of his spies or agents had seen Gerald in the Muddy Toad, informed Death, and Death then ordered the creature to be unleashed. Yet he had his doubts. Surely the mighty Death would have been able to find a way to get at him in the sanctuary had he wanted. Why wait? Afterall, Joggle and the voice were both able to come and go as they pleased. So why didn't Death?

He wondered briefly if it might have been the voice, but that made less sense than if Death had been after him. He had done what had been asked of him and he had been paid for it. Why bother paying him? And even if the voice had decided to kill him after paying him, why had it taken so long to try? There had been ample opportunities to kill him over the years. It made no sense to wait until now, and even less to send a dreamwalker.

His short list of suspects exhausted, Gerald was not sure he liked the emerging possibility that somewhere there was someone else, who he didn't know, who wanted him dead. Wanting to stifle this particularly uncomfortable hypothesis for as long as possible, his mind set to work in a vain attempt to explain why it was either Death or the voice who was now trying to kill him.

As he did so he wondered whether Death knew he was back in the city. He immediately regretted allowing that particular thought the space to take root in his tired mind. Unfortunately, though, once a thought like that is out in the world, it becomes very hard to ignore. Darl was right; the sooner they found out where the rose was the better.

If the dreamwalker's attack had been a spur, the thought that Death might already know he was in the city was like having his head submerged in an ice flow. The quicker he found the immortal's home the better, he decided. It was time to get to work.

Although he had been there before, he had seen very little of the city. He had been driven through the streets and delivered to the entrance of Death's home in a small driverless coach, which had waited for him to return with the rose before spiriting him away into the night. He had then been driven to a number of other locations, where a number of different transactions had been completed, all designed, he assumed, to ensure his employer received the rose and he got paid. He was also certain his mystery tour of the city had been designed to remove any chance of him making off with the rose, and definitely not allow the opportunity for him to make off with both the rose and his fee.

So, he set off to find the little black gate that had opened into the exquisitely maintained gardens with their wide gravel pathways, carefully crafted topiary, and beautiful flower beds filled with wild plants that gave off the most fantastic aromas. It was not the sort of garden he would have imagined belonging to Death. Not that he had ever imagined what Death's home might look like until he had broken into it. If he had, then he would have imagined it to be a little more minimalistic, but now he understood why an immortal would want to surround himself with beautiful things. It was the beauty of the sanctuary that had kept him sane for all the years he had been there. Something about the delicate intricacy of nature, its vivid colours and ceaseless motion, made the act of seeing it every day a good enough reason to exist.

He knew he would recognise those gardens the moment he set eyes upon them. The difficulty, of course, was that all he had seen of the entrance was the small wooden gate set into the long stone wall. There had been no distinguishing features, that he could remember. So, he reasoned, the sooner he began his search, the sooner he might be able to sleep at night without the fear of someone tearing him apart in his dreams or chopping him up in his bed.

Looking less like someone who had been living in a bush for a week, and occasionally stalked grannies, he decided to ask people passing by for directions to, what he was best able to articulate as, houses with big gardens. The question provoked a range of different responses, including suspicion, a thirty-minute history lesson on the growth of Tanglehaven, and some intensely political responses about the value of the wealthy to society. Gerald listened intently to the history lesson but backed away with a timid thank you from those who wanted to discuss the fairness of wealth distribution within the city. Not surprisingly the historian provided the most useful information.

With the sun starting to dip in the sky, he made his way towards the north wall where he understood the city's wealthiest merchants and officials lived. The sort of people who had the money to afford big houses with big gardens.

The contrast between the North Wall community and the rest of Tanglehaven was immediately obvious. A sizable park, by city standards, acted as a break between the community and the rest of the populace. As dusk drew down the dark to bring another day to a close Gerald saw well-dressed men and women walking hurriedly from the city, and presumably their places of work, across the park towards large houses where muted yellow lights already glowed within the windows. The park intrigued him. It was as though whoever had designed it had once visited the countryside, and quite liked it, but felt it could be improved upon by spacing the trees out a little more, cutting the grass regularly, and getting rid of any animals that either weren't on leads or didn't enjoy playing fetch.

On the other side of the park, he found clean streets and rows of massive stone houses that sat individually within their own grounds. In the growing dark they all looked the same, and by his meagre standards they would all be suitable homes for one of the most influential immortals in the world of mortals.

Gerald started to wonder if Death's neighbours knew who he was. Growing up he had always heard farm workers in the village saying that the people who ruled the world were in cahoots with the immortals. Judging by the wealth on display in the homes he saw in front of him, Gerald felt that the people who lived here almost undoubtedly had a say in how the world worked. He knew you didn't get a house like one of those by being a no one. He thought about whether he should start knocking on people's doors and asking if anyone knew which house belonged to Death, or if he could have a look around their gardens. Good sense got the better of him and he decided that was probably the quickest way to get himself forcibly removed by the Watchmen, who seemed a lot more visible on the streets around the park than they had been anywhere else in the city.

He made his way to the streets that ran behind the houses, but it appeared that none had any sort of entrance in the high walls that surrounded the gardens at the back of the homes. For a moment he thought this might be useful, after all, if there was only one home that had a little black gate into its garden, that would most likely be the house he was looking for. Unfortunately, there was a distinct lack of any gates in any walls and in all the time he wandered around he did not see a single one.

He continued his search until darkness had filled the streets, along with more officers of the Watch, who were starting to take an interest in him. Unable to think of a good enough reason for being there, and knowing the real reason would likely see him either arrested and spending the night at the Watch station, or arrested and spending a considerably longer period of time in the sort of place that provided help for people who were "looking for Death's house", or "wanted a cup of tea with the Mid-Winter Festival Goblin", he started to make his way back to the inn.

On his way back he walked along the side of a massive stone building that seemed to have ten, maybe even twenty, small streets leading to it, all disgorging people into a large square to its front. The square was rammed with people milling around. The number of people and the amount of noise they made seemed about normal for the market squares Gerald had passed through that day, except he could see no barrows, or stalls, or shops around the outside. He stood still for a minute looking around, trying to work out why so many people were attracted to this square. Although the side of the building he had walked down had been plain brick the front, by contrast, was a riot of sculpted figurines painted in bright colours. At first, they seemed almost chaotic in nature, but as he focused on the wall, which rose far higher than the three-storey stone houses he had seen along the north wall, he noticed that the figures appeared to be in little groups. Quite often those groups where repeated a number of times with the figures in different positions, or with different possessions, or with a different background. He realised that the groupings were meant to be scenes from stories, and they triggered a memory of going to the little temple in Spindle. The temple in Spindle had no figurines on its front walls, but the stories he had heard inside were the ones that seemed to be being played out by the figurines on the wall in front of him. He guessed that he had most probably found Tangleheaven's temple. He stood transfixed, lost in the beauty of the artwork and amazed by the immensity of the building.

Wanting to take it all in he slowly walked backwards through the press of the crowd until he noticed, in the darkness above, the start of a tower that rose out of the roof of the temple and into the night sky. It was not possible to tell how high the tower went. There was little light coming from the streets or the square, and the moon was hidden behind clouds that had dropped so low the tops of the city walls had disappeared. Despite that Gerald could just about make out more of the painted figures around the base of the tower.

Amazed by the art on display outside, he decided to take a look around inside. If it was half as beautiful as the outside, he reasoned, it would be well worth the time spent, and so he began to walk forward and allowed himself to become a part of the crowd flowing towards three of six large, open doors.

A small number of soldiers stood to attention by the doors, seemingly chosen for their height and shoulder width. They towered above the crowd clad in golden suits of plate armour with pristine white cloaks and hoods. They carried spears that seemed impractically long for fighting anywhere, let alone a crowded square, although Gerald also noticed far more practical broad bladed short swords hung at their waists.

As Gerald passed into the building, he saw rows and rows of pillars rising from floor to ceiling. The pillars were made of smooth white stone, and at the top where they met the roof, carvings of leaves, flowers, birds, and fairies covered in gold leaf hid the joints between the pillars and ceiling. The carvings ran from one pillar to the next, creating the impression of a canopy of golden trees and dividing the ceiling into giant squares. In each of those squares there was writing in letters of gold, red and black. Although Gerald could not read, he could appreciate the beauty of the calligraphy and the skill that would have gone into decorating each square. He wondered if they told the stories portrayed by the sculptures outside. He then wondered if Joggle would teach him to read one day.

The walls were heavily decorated with frescos and paintings presented in gilt frames depicting the many and various gods, and their often-tragic interactions with people. Gerald wasn't sure these images where necessarily the best choice if the intention was to present the gods in such a way as to make them adored by the people, but he'd never heard anyone else raise this particular concern. He would be the first to concede that he had never really understood religion, despite his mum's best efforts. So, he shrugged his shoulders and simply enjoyed the art for the talent that had created it, rather than any messages the artist may, or may not, have been trying to convey.

It appeared that no space had been left unfilled by images of divine beings, or unfortunate mortals. He found himself thinking that if an art collection was a reflection of piety, then this temple had to be one of the holiest places in the world. As he ventured further inside, he noticed that the crowd seemed to break naturally into two groups. Around three walls of the massive temple room preachers were stationed at regular intervals. The fourth wall was taken up with the six large doors allowing ingress and egress to and from the building. The preachers stood on great stone blocks with steps chiselled into the sides of them to allow access. People entered through three doors on one side of the temple and gravitated towards the centre of the room. They then walked around listening to the different sermons until they heard one of interest, at which point they would break away from the flow of worshippers and join the congregation gathered around their chosen speaker. If they reached the end of the hall and had not found a sermon that took their fancy the crowd turned back on itself. It then flowed back up the hall to hear what the preachers along the opposite wall had to offer.

Gerald found the whole situation most strange. He thought about the momentary connection he had felt with the old gods at the lake and wondered if anyone could make a similar connection in all the noise and movement. He kept to the centre of the building, moving with the crowd until he saw a particularly animated man throwing himself around his stone. He was yelling at the top of his lungs about blood, and punishment, and death. Yet, for all his enthusiasm it did not appear that his message had particularly resonated with any of the worshippers, and so his fervour was only being witnessed by the crowd as it shuffled by.

In his peripheral vision Gerald noticed some activity close to the stone where the unpopular preacher rallied against sin and the enemies of the gods. A tall picture several feet from the preacher, which Gerald now realised was about the height and width of the sort of door you would find in pretty much any normal size building, swung open. A guard, without his spear, accompanied by a smaller man dressed in a thick grey robe came out. The guard approached the animated speaker and motioned for him to step down. The preacher stopped his monologue immediately and complied with the guard's request with surprising speed, and without any argument or remonstration. The smaller man in the grey robe then climbed the stairs to the stone and started to speak.

Almost before the smaller man climbed the steps, some of those in the central flow of people had broken off and started to form a congregation in anticipation of his words. Despite the preacher's apparent celebrity, Gerald was not tempted to join the crowd, and continued his tour around the temple until he inevitably found himself at one of the doors that served as an exit and was disgorged into the night.

Outside he felt a sharp snap of coldness in the air which he wasn't dressed for, and decided it was time to return to the inn.

Chapter 13

As he walked away from the temple the crowds quickly thinned out. Gerald soon found himself alone in empty streets trying to find his way home. By luck, more than judgement, he made a series of turns that put him on a path towards the city gate they had entered by that morning, and soon he began to see streets and locked up shops he recognised.

Gerald felt the hairs on the back of his neck rise. He looked around, but there was no one to be seen. There was something about cities he found unnerving. The feeling of being surrounded by people and yet completely disconnected from everyone, all at the same time. At this very moment he was in the midst of thousands, maybe even tens of thousands of people, some only metres away, and yet he felt as alone and vulnerable as he had in the middle of the forest. The city was resting in its homes, behind walls within its walls. Each house, a little castle in its own right, had its drawbridge up, protecting those inside against the things that lurked in dark corners and shadowed streets, leaving those who remained outside to fend for themselves.

The feeling that he was being watched grew. He slowed his pace, and as he walked through the middle of a small square with streets leading from it on each side he stopped.

"You may as well come out. We both know you're watching me," he said loudly, tone somewhere between confidence and resignation. He moved his hand to the hilt of his knife and listened for the slightest sound that might betray the direction his assailant would come from.

The skittering sound of footsteps came first. Light, but quick. It sounded like there might be several of them, although he hoped that was just an echo bouncing off the cobbles, and the buildings that watched blindly on either side of each street. Then came the sound of material dragging on the ground. He stood, unflinching, trying to decide what he should do next, all the while wondering why he wasn't running as fast as he could towards the inn. Then he realised the rushing footsteps were coming from the street in front of him, the direction he needed to take to get home.

Suddenly he found he had crossed the fine line where unflinching became frozen, and fear gripped him. He had expected the attack to come from behind, quick, and hopefully painless. Coming from the front made Gerald worry that the attacker wanted to look him in the eyes, probably wanted to see him suffer. His brain overrode his earlier bravado and his bladder felt ready to overrun.

A hooded figure appeared from the street in front of him, and upon seeing him it increased its speed. His knife was now in his hand, although he wasn't entirely sure how it had happened, and he was waving it at the apparition like one might wave a kipper at a tiger. The newly discovered part of him that had made such a mess of the dark wolf seemed to have taken over. It forced him to adopt what it thought was a fighting stance. It was a strange feeling, he found he had time to reflect, readying himself for a fight. The world seemed to slow down as the thing got closer to him. He wondered if he was starting to get the hang of combat now. For a split second he allowed himself to consider what he would see if he looked down upon himself. Images of heroic warriors were dragged from his memory, although he could not have looked more different from them in reality. Standing alone in a pose that, to experienced fighters, telegraphed the fact that he had never been in a fight before whilst day dreaming was certainly not the way he was going to earn his place in the legends, at least not the ones where the hero survives.

As the figure covered the last few steps between them everything sped up again, and Gerald felt himself lock up. It stopped just short of the tip of his knife and a familiar voice said, "Boo."

Darl lowered the hood of her cloak. "Relax, it's me," she said, hands materialising from folds of dark green cloth, pushing the knife blade to one side.

"By the angels, you almost scared the life out of me," Gerald stuttered, heart racing as he returned the knife to its sheath.

"Who did you think I was?" Darl asked, a smile on her lips.

"Death." Gerald replied earnestly.

"What?" Darl said with the start of a laugh in her voice which stopped the moment she realised he was serious. "You think that Death is after you?"

"Well, yeah, I mean I stole from him," Gerald said, whilst trying to calm himself down.

"What, you think that the literal embodiment of dying, arguably one of the most powerful of all the immortals, would sneak up on you in the night like a common footpad? That's not how he works. Believe me. If Death wanted you, he would have taken you already. And you certainly wouldn't have had time to fumble around with your knife," Darl replied firmly.

"Even though I'm immortal?" Gerald questioned, unconvinced despite the certainty in her voice.

"Immortals can die too you know. And he's every bit as involved," Darl replied.

"So, you don't think he's after me then?" Gerald asked.

"No," she replied. "At least not right now."

"What's that meant to mean?" Gerald asked, not sure Darl's response was making him feel any better.

"I understand that right now you're trying to come to terms with a lot but jumping at every shadow you come across won't help. Yes, you might have stolen from him, but has it not occurred to you that just as you didn't know you were stealing from him, he doesn't know it was you doing the stealing? I mean you said it yourself, you walked into his house, took the rose, and left. You didn't set off any alarms, you weren't chased by guards. You just walked in and walked out again."

"It was over pretty quickly," Gerald chipped in, with just a hint of smugness.

"Gerald, I know that sometimes you think we treat you like a child, and we do, but don't for one second think we don't know that there's something about you that's just, well... different," Darl tried her best to explain. "You were chosen to steal from Death. There must have been a reason for that. So just like we don't know the reason why you were chosen I think we also have to accept there is other stuff we don't know. The best way I know to deal with a load of unkowns is just to lay them to one side and work with what you do know. At the moment, we have no reason to suspect Death has any idea about you, or us, or what we're up to. But we do know there's a demon on your trail, and I'm going to guess that your real concern is about who sent the dreamwalker."

Gerald nodded, and Darl continued, "As much as, I'm guessing, you don't want to consider that there is someone you don't know after you, we can't just discount the possibility. The good news, though, is that getting the demon woman maybe the key to finding out who it is. We know that demons generally only do things because they're being paid, and they're expensive. Whoever hired her most likely has a lot of resources to draw on, so it makes sense that if they had the resources to employ her, they're likely to have the resources to enslave dreamwalkers."

"So, the old woman we chased this afternoon is definitely a demon?" Gerald asked.

"Chag's sure of it, which is good enough for me," Darl said.

"I'm confused. I thought the old man summoned the demon?" Gerald asked.

"Absolutely. The old man almost certainly summoned her, but he isn't controlling her, and he won't be the person who originally sent her after you. I think the fact that him and his dad nursed such a massive grudge against you was just a happy coincidence for her," Darl said. "We've been discussing it all afternoon, whilst you were doing... whatever it was you've been up to."

"So, you think if we can stop her, we can also stop the dreamwalker?" Gerald asked, welcoming this particular line of thought.

"It's possible. It does mean you'll need to act as bait again, but hopefully just for another day. We have a plan," Darl said confidently.

"Sure, I'm happy to spend another day with Chag if that's what it's going to take," Gerald replied, feeling surprisingly relaxed about Darl's suggestion.

Darl took a deep breath, "Unfortunately Chag can't be involved."

"What?" Gerald shot back rapidly reconsidering his earlier appraisal of the plan.

"Today she almost got caught. She's not going to like that at all. It's going to make her really cautious. If we send you out with Chag again, she's going to be extra careful about what she does, and we need her to go the other way. We need her to think she has got the upper hand again. You guys trapped her today because she was careless, she took her eye off Chag. We need her to be careless again."

"So how do we do that?" Gerald asked.

"We need her to believe that we think we scared her off today. We want her to think that we're convinced we've turned the tables on her, and we're no longer worried about what she's up to," Darl explained. "That means we need you to be seen out and about again, without Chag."

"Well, I do need to pick up some clothes tomorrow," Gerald replied nervously.

"More new clothes?" Darl asked, taking a step back to get a better view of Gerald's new ensemble.

"Yes," Gerald replied defensively, as he felt he was going to have to defend his decision to abandon the filth caked clothes he had worn on the journey from Spindle-Upon-Spindle. "But I didn't just spend the afternoon shopping, I spent most of the time trying to find Death's home."

"What," Darl exclaimed, the smallest hint of anger in her voice. "We're meant to be doing that together, after the demon is dealt with."

"I know, but I thought it would be helpful to make a start. Besides, even if I had found the place, I wasn't planning on knocking on the door and introducing myself," Gerald replied sheepishly.

"Okay, I understand," Darl said, trying her best not to sound like an irate parent. "Tomorrow morning you need to be out and visible. Do whatever you want, but whatever you do don't give her any ideas about what we're actually up to. This is about us trying to get one over on her, not the other way around."

"No problem, I think I have a suitably roundabout way to continue searching without making what we're up to obvious. I'll need to take Joggle with me though." Gerald replied hopefully.

Darl thought for a second, "Okay, but you only have the morning. Then you need to be back at the inn."

Somewhere in the distance the sound of a Watchman announcing that all was well disturbed their deliberations. Darl listened to the distant proclamation and looked around. She had been excited about finding Gerald and had momentarily forgotten why she had been out in the street in the first place. The little rush of excitement had now passed. "I think we should find the others and get back to the inn, otherwise you'll be adding Chag to the list of people wanting to kill you," Darl said, a little too seriously for Gerald's liking. She took him by the hand and together they made their way back towards the inn.

Chapter 14

Still sitting in the darkness of the warehouse office, now in her demon form, Jade took the runeblade she had recovered the day she had returned to Spindle out from one of the hidden pockets in her shoulder bag. It was wrapped tightly in cloth and bound with leather straps. She unwrapped it and turned it over slowly in her hands, admiring the workmanship just as she did every time she gazed upon it. It was in many ways an unremarkable weapon, a knife that looked like any other knife that could be bought in any market or at any smithy. The only difference was the weak blue glow from the runes carved into its blade, that were only visible when it was in the presence of an immortal.

She hated the thing because she believed that the blade hated her. It was an annoying necessity, and one of the reasons she never knowingly accepted commissions that involved immortals. It was not the only reason though. Killing immortals wasn't necessarily any more difficult to do with the right tools than killing mortals; but killing an immortal tended to lead to a lot more complications. Mortals had a limited time in the world, and so there was a limit to the number of friends they could make or the amount of close family they had; in essence, there was a limit on the number of people who might want to investigate or avenge their deaths. It was very rare that a desire for revenge in mortals extended further than a generation, or maybe two in the case of humans due to their short lifespans.

The friends and family of immortals were, in the main, also immortal. That meant the timeframe for revenge became somewhat longer. Perhaps more significantly, though, was that immortals generally had a lot more time on their hands than mortals, making an investigation, at the very least, much more likely, if only as a result of a prolonged period of boredom.

There was also the practical aspect of carrying the runeblade. She enjoyed the comfortable onesidedness of being an immortal who made their living from hunting down mortals. It wasn't that she wasn't handy in a fight; it was just that she much preferred fighting when she knew that whatever the outcome was, she would walk away alive. Having to use the runeblade changed the situation. She was now carrying a weapon that could kill her quarry but also allow them to kill her if they managed to get hold of it. Of course, no matter whom she was after, she always went out of her way to stack the odds in her favour, but odds should never be confused with certainties.

Jade also felt annoyed with herself that the moleman had got the better of her again. She tried to make herself feel a little better by telling herself that she now knew that Gerald had come to the city to retrieve something, but she reflected that this might have been a part of the ruse to get her to follow them. There could be any number of reasons as to why they were here.

Jade may have had as much pride as the next demon, but she knew the importance of not immediately blaming someone else for her failures and ignoring her own shortcomings. That being said, she was a firm believer in balance, so whenever she did acknowledge her own shortcomings, she would also acknowledge the responsibility other people should take for her failures. In this case, though, she had to grudgingly accept that she had taken her eye off him for too long and paid the price.

She contemplated the events of the afternoon. Her mind began to swim with thoughts and theories. Snatches of overheard and misremembered conversations drifted between her conscious and subconscious. She was tired - tired and angry, with a wound to her ego that needed soothing. She needed to rest.

She wrapped and bound the runeblade once more and returned it to the hidden pocket in her shoulder bag. She cleared some space on the floor where she could meditate and sat cross-legged, head up, looking into nothingness. She closed her eyes and took a deep breath in through her nose. She focused on the breath as it travelled into her lungs before dispersing throughout her body. She breathed out. The world and all her worries felt a million miles away now, condensed into a distant point of light at the furthest edge of her vision, to be returned to only when she was ready.

In the depths of her subconscious her memories started to stir. Words overheard, and knowledge taken by interrogation that she had not understood the relevance of, or not been interested in at that moment, drifted around lazily. Further down, memories of stories lost to time roused, pushing themselves up to swim amongst the words, occasionally bumping into them. Mostly when they struck each other, they flew apart, but sometimes they connected, and slowly the connections increased as a single thought started to take shape.

At about four o'clock the next morning Jade's eyes snapped open. Tiny yellow pupils set in dark orbs stared out across the gloom. She shuddered. It wasn't an instinct or a gut feel. It was far more than that. As an immortal, Jade had memories that spanned the lifetime of the world and beyond. As a demon, she was not able to instantly recall everything she remembered. When she rested, her subconscious would process the problems at the forefront of her mind, and present to her consciousness everything she knew that was connected to those concerns. That way she awoke physically rested and mentally prepared for the challenges that she knew would be ahead of her.

She remained sitting, bolt upright, as whispered conversations by campfires, the wittering of the old man and stories from the Lost Lands stitched themselves together. The resulting picture was not good. Although not complete she began to see something that potentially connected Gerald to all those things. It was the Rose of Amzharr. Had he stolen the Rose of Amzharr? If it was true, she could be in a lot of trouble.

The theft itself wasn't an issue to her; after all, people stole stuff all the time and to her the rose was basically just stuff. But she had been paid to kill him, and whilst she knew almost nothing about the voice that had employed her, the one thing she did know about it - because demons can tell these things - was that the voice came from a mortal. And there was an inevitability that when a mortal wanted people killed, and that rose was involved, it was all about that rose. She had, she began to worry, been pulled into a mortal's scheme to take possession of it and that was a bad thing indeed for an immortal. There were few things that all immortals agreed on, but one of those few things was that you should never help mortals get their grubby little paws on the Rose of Amzharr.

Chapter 15

Gerald set out with Joggle the next morning on their mission for him to be seen to be letting his guard down. When they had all finally returned to the inn the previous evening, Gerald had apologised for his afternoon wanderings and told them about his time spent searching for Death's home. At some point the conversation took an unexpected twist. Having explained the frustrating lack of gates and worrying number of Watchmen around the north wall that had impeded his search, Joggle had interrupted. The irk had asked if it was possible that Death did not actually live in the city and if the gate, wherever it was, was actually some kind of portal between the city and Death's home. Gerald became instantly defensive, before doubling down on his assertion that Death *definitely* lived in the city, as Joggle started to talk about Gerald's *belief* that Death lived in the city.

"And what is your *belief* based on?" the little creature had snapped after Gerald had disregarded his suggestion.

Gerald had replied that it was based on him coming to the city, going through Death's garden gate, and spending time in the property. He had then described the journey through the city streets in the small carriage, and the little black gate set into the long brick wall. He described the gardens and the house in as much detail as he could remember, even making a number of surprisingly detailed sketches in an effort to really ram his point home. Joggle then pointed out that whilst the drawings were all very useful and proved that the gate, like any good gate, served as a link between two places, they did not prove that both of those places were actually in the city. After that Joggle became very metaphysical, at which point Gerald lost all understanding of what was being said, as well as all interest, and refused to say anything more on the subject to the irk.

Joggle had at one point appealed to Darl for support. Not wishing to get involved in this particular tête-à-tête, she had said it didn't matter that much for the moment since their priority was getting their hands on the demon. He had then appealed to Chag, who had grunted something about technicalities before shuffling off to find something more interesting in an empty corner of the room, pipe gripped firmly between his teeth.

The argument had flared up again the next morning over breakfast. However, despite Gerald still failing to understand the point that Joggle was making, they found themselves agreeing that Gerald's plan for the morning would resolve their argument. Darl and Chag listened to the pair bickering in the room, like parents who no longer had the energy to intervene in their children's arguments and had resigned themselves to letting them run their course, if only because neither child was trying to stuff their favourite toys up the other one's nose at that particular moment. It also helped that they were about to be allowed out to play, giving Darl and Chag some much sought-after peace and quiet.

With the argument put on hold, because both expected to be vindicated by about lunchtime, Gerald and Joggle set off through the busy city streets. After a brief stop to collect Gerald's new clothes, they made their way towards the Temple of Speakers, which Joggle had informed Gerald was the name of the building he had visited the night before.

At first, Joggle had attempted to make his way through the streets on foot, too proud to accept a lift from the lad following their surprisingly bitter row. However, as the number of people in the city streets swelled, he soon decided that his place on the lad's shoulder was far safer than attempting to dodge feet and barrow wheels on the cobbled streets. He made his way up Gerald's leg and onto his perch. Joggle then had a one-sided discussion about whether this position was either too conspicuous or not conspicuous enough, whilst Gerald kept an eye out for pistol toting old ladies. After far more toing and froing than should have ever been necessary for that particular conversation, even by Joggle's standards, the irk decided it was probably the right level of conspicuousness to ensure they attracted the demon's attention, but not suspicious enough that she might think they were trying to lead her into another trap. At that point Gerald suggested that he probably shouldn't be saying anything about traps out loud, because that was the easiest way for any demons that might be listening to work out what they were really up to. Joggle conceded and stopped talking for what he felt was a protracted period of time. A few seconds later he started up again, this time providing Gerald with a running commentary of anything he noticed going on around him that he knew anything about. It was an intriguing litany of facts and opinions, albeit opinions were presented as facts, that Gerald found himself tuning in and out of, depending upon the subject.

Gerald was always amazed that despite the near continuous outpouring of verbiage, Joggle was always very aware of his surroundings. Gerald guessed that this must have been some sort of survival trait; surely a creature that small that talked so much would be an easy meal for any half-decent predator? Gerald then started to wonder if Joggle had a natural predator, and if so, whether it would be polite to ask what it might be.

Joggle had to admit he was impressed, although very quietly, with the way the lad navigated the streets, quickly finding the tailors before heading towards the Temple of Speakers. It was as though he knew the city like the back of his hand, despite having spent so little time in it. He weaved around other pedestrians, market stalls and occasional street entertainers as though he had been doing it all his life. To cap it all, and much to Joggle's delight, whenever they passed street vendors selling nuts, the odd one or two managed to find their way from the vendors' trays to Joggle, and the irk grinned as he nibbled away between sentences.

For the first time since arriving in the city Gerald noticed that the temple, or at least the tower that rose above it, was visible from almost everywhere. It rose high into the sky, piercing the clouds like a pillar supporting the heavens. Despite its visibility Gerald did not head directly towards it. Instead, he chose a slightly more circuitous route, intended to give the impression to anyone following him that, whilst he was aware they may be following him, he wasn't overly concerned about it.

Jade had been waiting across the street from the inn that morning when they left and followed them at a discreet distance. She was trying her best not to dwell on the events of the previous day, whilst looking out for the moleman in case he was somewhere behind her again.

Jade had spent a lot of time debating what to do following the previous day's incident. The debate had come to an abrupt end the moment she had awoken with the concern that, whatever Gerald and his bunch of misfits were up to, the rose might be involved. She knew she could not be the immortal who had been involved, no matter how indirectly, in a plot to steal it and then not be involved in recovering it. So, early that morning she had found a sufficiently discreet vantage point overlooking the entrance to the inn and begun her watch. She had felt oddly reassured to see Gerald leave at a reasonable time in the morning, accompanied by the glorified squirrel, and seemingly no one else. She began to wonder if this meant that they thought they had scared her off yesterday. Of course, it didn't mean the moleman wasn't lurking around somewhere else, so as she followed Gerald and the irk through the streets, she checked regularly to see if there was any sign of him. Unbeknownst to Gerald, Jade's distraction, because she was so concerned about the moleman, meant she was in no position to realise that he was doing his absolute best to be noticed, and make it easy for her to follow him.

They reached the temple square just before lunchtime. The crowds were milling around preachers who stood on upturned crates, in a parody of what Gerald had seen the night before inside the temple. The preachers in the square were very different. Whereas the speakers in the temple had been dressed in identical, clean, grey robes with full, round bellies overhanging golden cords that encircled their waists, the preachers outside lacked uniformity, in most cases basic hygiene and, in the odd case, clothes. Many wore tired robes of varying colours with mud, and possibly blood, dried into them. Those that had hair wore it long and unkempt, with tiny charms and trinkets woven into it. They spoke in different languages, calling on different gods and immortals, and their sermons were more explosive, more extreme, and more animated than those within the temple. Each speaker did what they could to outperform the person to either side of them. The only thing they all had in common was the small container that sat at their feet where the odd coin lay.

Gerald pushed through the crowd that milled around the preachers. It was not easy going. The crowd in the temple flowed around the pillars, allowing a gentle ingress and egress to and from each preacher. There was a satisfying sense of order to it. That order did not exist in the square. Around the preachers stood tiny congregations made up of individuals, each responding to the preachers in their own way. Some listened, some were deep in prayer, others shouted in agreement, or loudly declared charges of false witness or bloody-minded stupidity. But regardless of what anyone in the congregations said or did, the preachers continued, voices screaming at the skies and arms raised seemingly simultaneously in praise and anger. Around the congregations, other people moved heading in any number of directions. It was chaotic, confused and claustrophobic. Gerald realised that being in a crowd like this would make him almost impossible to follow, and so he made his way to the nearest side street, and from there found his way into one of the alleys that ran along the plain side wall of the temple.

If Gerald had found progress through the crowd challenging, Jade's passage had been near impossible. One of the disadvantages, she was realising, of choosing a form that made her look so vulnerable in a fight was that those vulnerabilities also worked against her in other physically demanding situations, particularly where a characterful disguise needed to be maintained. This was one of those situations. Returning to her natural seven-foot tall, bright green, winged self may have made progress through the crowd easier, but it was also the quickest way she knew to blow her cover. So, Jade persevered in her diminutive human form with the large shoulder bag. She resorted to using her stick to stab at people's feet to encourage them to be anywhere but in her way, and a sweet old lady smile by way of explanation and apology when someone realised it was her stick that had stabbed them. She lost sight of Gerald a couple of times, but as soon as she realised that he was not heading inside the temple, she broke away from the crowd and ran around the side streets in search of him.

Gerald stopped and looked around him as though he was bothered that someone might be watching.

"Right, mate, you're up," he whispered to Joggle. "Do you remember what you're looking for?"

"I have an eidetic memory," Joggle replied sharply, affronted by Gerald's question, and not completely comfortable with being referred to as mate. He liked Gerald but wasn't sure their relationship had reached that particular milestone of informality just yet.

Jade sneaked a look around the corner of one of the many alleys that ran into the streets surrounding the temple. She congratulated herself on her excellent understanding of her prey and her ability to remain one step ahead of them, as she watched Gerald and the irk. It sounded as though they were bickering about something, which seemed to be the natural state of things when the irk spent a protracted amount of time with anyone. Eventually, the irk stopped talking and she watched as the little creature leapt from Gerald's shoulder, onto the temple wall and scampered upwards.

The temple consisted of two sections. The first was the main building where the preachers spoke. This was basically a large, upturned brick box with no windows. Whilst the front of the building was highly decorated with sculpture and six massive iron-bound, dark wood doors, the side and rear walls were bare. It was only their size that gave any indication that they belonged to a building of any significance. Fortunately, the bricks were sufficiently old and weather-beaten to allow Joggle's claws easy enough purchase to make his way quickly onto the roof. From there the going became much easier.

The second section was a wide, cylindrical tower that sprouted from the centre of the flat roof. The tower rose high into the sky. Joggle stood in an awed silence as he took in the detailed carvings that covered every inch of the tower's surface, as well as the stone creatures that emerged or hung from it at irregular intervals. He marvelled not only at the combined feat of engineering and art, but also at how much fun it would be to climb.

He climbed for quite a distance until he stopped and looked down to see the maze of streets spreading out in every direction across the city. At the height at which he stopped, he estimated he was barely a quarter of the way up, although he could not see to the top of the tower and so had no reference point with which to support his supposition. What amazed him most was that the further he climbed, the more detailed and ornate the carvings became. He wondered if there was some form of magical protection around the tower to prevent it from weathering, as each image looked so fresh and sharp it could have been carved that morning. He also noticed that despite an abundance of places for birds to rest or roost, there seemed to be a distinct lack of flying creatures around the tower, and certainly no evidence that they frequented the skies directly above it. His inquisitive nature had made him want to scratch at the stone or try and break a nose off one of the many faces that looked out across the city, but he resisted in case whatever preserved the artwork did so with a lethal force. As far-fetched as it sounded, it would explain the lack of birds in the skies directly above the temple.

He clambered around the north side of the tower and looked out towards the part of the city where Gerald had said Death's house would most likely be. Joggle could see, from where he was, the parks and the houses laid out in a convenient patchwork. He could also see beyond the walls and out into the forest.

There were certainly some large houses with well-kempt gardens, but none of the gardens were of the size or scale that Gerald had spoken of the previous evening. Joggle also noted that the garden style Gerald had described was clearly not the current fashion, so he also looked for properties of sufficient scale to match the house that Gerald had sketched, but there was nothing that seemed capable of fitting those massive dimensions.

With no property corresponding to Gerald's descriptions to the north, Joggle darted around the tower. The city's history was visible in the streets below. He could see how the city had spread from the furthest north corner, where the oldest buildings and stretches of walls formed a self-contained keep, down to where it met the sea in the south-east, where a busy port and warehouse district had sprung up. It was even possible to see where houses had grown up around the old walls, which had then had new walls built around them as they had become sufficiently permanent to be accepted into the sprawling organism of brick and bodies that was Tanglehaven. But regardless of how the city had grown or where he looked, he could not find anything that suggested the house that Gerald had visited was within the city.

An hour and a half later Joggle returned to the alley where Gerald waited patiently.

"Well?" Gerald asked hopefully.

"Nothing," Joggle replied, suppressing the "I told you so" that wanted to explode from his mouth.

"I don't understand. The place was massive," Gerald said, sounding disappointed. "Did you go high enough?"

"I got high enough to be able to see beyond the walls in every direction," Joggle replied, offended again by the implication that he had got wrong the highly complex tasks of climbing up something and looking for something really big.

"I don't get it," Gerald said, frustrated. "Maybe I need to have a look."

"And that will change things how?" Joggle asked, raising an eyebrow.

"I know what I'm looking for," Gerald retorted.

"Feel free," snapped Joggle. "I'll just wait here."

Gerald took a deep breath and looked up at the featureless wall in front of him. He rubbed his hands together with a determination that he immediately realised surpassed his climbing ability. "Okay, fine," he said begrudgingly. "But I definitely went through that gate in this city."

"I'm not debating that," Joggle said calmly. "Just don't be so hard on yourself. For what it's worth I do believe the gate is in this city somewhere, and we will find it. That being said, getting... you know who... is our priority for now."

"I suppose," Gerald said, slightly crestfallen that the one thing he thought he would have been able to do for the party had not come to fruition.

Jade did her best to watch the exchange between Gerald and the irk whilst remaining out of sight, which also meant she was unable to hear them talking. Unaware of what they had set out to do that day, her mind went into overdrive. Levers were pulled, cogs clicked and pushed each other around, all the while deepening her suspicions. What if, she wondered, the irk and the moleman had been involved in the theft somehow? The first theft. They would have both been alive. What if the three of them had

130

conspired together to steal the rose? What if they had hidden it in the city somewhere, hoping to return someday and claim their prize? What if that someday was today?

Chapter 16

Jade was now fully committed to finding out exactly what the party was up to. She spent an uncomfortable afternoon and night on the roof of a building that overlooked the entry to the inn. Gerald and the irk had returned to the place as soon as they had left the temple. She had thought about trying to find out which room they were staying in but, in the end, decided she could not risk being seen. She had then tried throughout the night, when it became apparent the party were in no rush to leave again, moving between the roofs around the inn in the hope that she would be able to find a view into their room, but by then all the curtains and shutters around the first floor were closed. So, she ended up exactly where she had started her vigil the previous afternoon.

To add to the general discomfort of being on an exposed roof top for almost eighteen hours, brooding clouds had settled over the city at around three o'clock in the morning. A few minutes later heavy, cold drops of rain started to fall, soaking her clothes, pasting her white hair over her eyes, and turning the roof tops into slippery, shiny surfaces.

The rain eased off at about six o'clock for an hour or so, before returning much heavier than before, this time with a sharp north wind that turned Jade's cold wet clothes to freezing wet clothes. Although as a demon she felt these things as facts rather than sensations, she spent so much of her time in her human form that she had taught herself over the years to react to things in the same way as the person she imitated would. Over a long period of time that behaviour had become almost instinctive; and having been particularly fond of her current incarnation she had spent many years as her, so many that she now found herself shivering uncontrollably as she sat on the roof. The whole experience was pretty miserable.

She had lost track of time and, she had convinced herself, all feeling in her toes, when Chag and Gerald emerged. They wore heavy woollen cloaks with hoods that they left down as they exited the inn. They stood for a while talking, before disappearing in opposite directions. She considered for a moment whether to follow Gerald. Unfortunately, her position on the roof made following anyone out of the question, unless they were prepared to give her half an hour to make her way down to the street and find a dry set of clothes, which the current situation certainly didn't allow for.

It turned out to be of little consequence as both returned within an hour, the moleman laden with provisions and Gerald with a rather suspicious-looking donkey. Jade tried her best to work out why the donkey looked suspicious, but for the life of her she couldn't quite put her finger on it. She had a feeling though, as much as someone can who doesn't spend much time around donkeys, that if you were going on a long journey this would not be the donkey you would choose. However, she also suspected that as Gerald had done the acquiring, and was apparently some kind of thief, it had been acquired on the basis of availability as opposed to whatever a high standard measurement of donkeyness was.

The moleman's reaction certainly reinforced Jade's view that this was not the sort of donkey you could ever get excited about, leastways as far as she could get excited about donkeys. Despite the condition of the animal the moleman began to pack provisions onto the odd little beast, whilst Gerald disappeared inside. He reappeared moments later with the barmaid. With all her time in the city focused on following Gerald and avoiding the moleman, Jade had all but forgotten about her.

She did not look in a good way. Gerald held her by her right arm, supporting and guiding her to the awaiting donkey. Like the others she wore a woollen cloak with the hood down, which Gerald pulled up as the rain started to fall again. Her face was pale and drawn. Dark shadows hung beneath her eyes, and she moved slowly, uncertainly. Jade wondered if she could even see the world around her, such was the caution in her movement and the extent to which Gerald seemed to guide her. The barmaid clutched her left arm to her chest; it was heavily bandaged. She was a shade of the woman who had entered the city and Jade wondered if the bite from the dark wolf had become infected. She had heard terrible things could happen to wounds if they weren't treated properly. Maybe the irk was not as adept in medical matters as he had made out in the forest.

It took a while to get the woman comfortable on the donkey. Once she was secure and the moleman was happy the creature wasn't over-burdened, they headed slowly towards the city gates. Knowing the party would have to traverse the wide-open stretch of grassland, before they disappeared into the ring of trees that surrounded the city, Jade took the opportunity to change forms. She climbed down from the roof and ducked off into the side streets in search of a dark alley or abandoned building she could transform in. She decided it would be easiest to keep track of the party from the air, using the low rain clouds to remain out of sight.

It did not take her long to find a burnt-out worker's cottage in the shadow of the south wall. She allowed her wings to flex free of her human cocoon. She let them carry her straight up into the sky as she prayed, to no one in particular, that she had gone unnoticed in the brief few seconds it took her to change and take to the skies.

As predicted, the party was making their way beneath the main gate by the time she reached the safety of the clouds. She was moving far faster than them, and so assuming that they were intending to head back towards the sanctuary, she flew high and found a suitably large tree that overlooked the route she expected them to take. However, as the party made their way down the hill back to where the road forked, they did not follow the road they had come in on. They turned instead to travel in the opposite direction. Jade watched with interest as they slowly walked away from her.

The group followed the road through the cleared grassland, before disappearing from sight between the great trees of the forest. Jade opened her wings and flew above the clouds, intending to alight inside the part of the woods they had just disappeared into. She wanted to change back to her human form, and once again follow them from a safe distance on foot.

She heard screaming. It was the woman's voice, which she recognised from the night of the wolf attack. Hearing the urgency of her screeches, suddenly joined by the sound of metal clashing through the trees, Jade's instincts kicked in. Without thinking she plunged down through the clouds, directly towards the noise, expecting to see bandits or wolves attacking the party.

Just as she was about to break through the canopies of the ancient oaks, she felt a stillness in the air. It was as though the world had stopped. She watched helplessly, mid-dive, as a wave of azure energy, solid as a brick wall and warm as a summer's day moved towards her. It crashed into her and rolled through her. She dropped. Darkness overcame her as she felt the solid thud of the ground beneath her.

Chapter 17

Jade came around slowly. She was groggy and making sense of her surroundings took time. She had no idea what had hit her, but it had hit her hard. Her ears were ringing, and her vision was blurred. Being unable to see or hear, her body gave her the first indications of where she had ended up. She noticed that she was in her demon form because she could feel her wings, and to a lesser extent her tail. She tried her best to swear but couldn't be sure whether she had actually made a sound, and if so, whether that sound had been roughly word-shaped or just a loosely defined grunt. She felt her wings first; she assumed this was because they had been unceremoniously pulled around a rough cylindrical object and bound in a fashion which, either suggested someone knew how to stop demons flying away, or someone had too much time and too much rope on their hands. She suspected it was most likely the former. She guessed she had been tied to either a pillar or a tree, but her short-term memory had been scrambled and she preferred not to make any assumptions about where she was - that could get you in trouble. A rush of feeling returned to the rest of her body, and it was not long before she realised that she had been tied in a sitting position with her legs straight out in front of her. Her vision then started to clear, and she was able to take in her surroundings. She was bound to a tree in a small clearing. Something snapped inside her. She remembered the blue wave, she remembered falling and crashing through leafy canopies. Her memory was coming back.

She took a series of deep breaths before cursing her stupidity for falling into yet another trap. She recalled the scene as she hit the ground, a glimpse of the barmaid sitting on the donkey screaming at nothing, whilst the moleman knocked his short sword against his buckler, a look of boredom on his face. She would have found the whole scene mildly amusing if she hadn't been the butt of the joke. It was becoming a bit of a habit that she really needed to break. She really couldn't be this stupid? Could she?

She pulled herself together, lying to herself that she had been in far worse situations before. She swept the distracting thoughts from her mind, telling herself she needed to focus on what was in front of her if she was to have any chance of surviving. Her chief concern was that she was trapped in her demon form. If her captors knew what she was, which she was fairly certain the moleman would, there was a good chance they would know her vulnerabilities. If they knew that and they bothered to search her belongings thoroughly, they would likely be able to have a reasonable guess as to what the rune scrolled blade, wrapped up and secreted inside her bag, was for. And it was for this exact reason she hated having to carry the damned runeblade.

At least if she had been in human form, they might have tried to torture her or kill her with normal weapons, which she would have greatly preferred. Not only because they would not have actually hurt, but also because she would get the chance to play dead, which Jade had found over the years was the quickest way to get people to lose interest in sticking sharp, and occasionally blunt, metal objects into her.

It wasn't long before the cold and damp of the forest floor started creeping through her clothes. Jade sighed. The irritating sensation signalled her return to full consciousness. She looked around in the gloom of twilight. Being a creature of the Abyss, the lack of light didn't affect her; but it did give her a fighting chance when it came to guessing how long she had been out for. She was not surprised in the least when her eyes finally settled on the moleman. He was standing in front of her, dressed head to toe in chainmail, holding her runeblade in one hand and her mace in the other.

"Afternoon," he said in the same gravelly monotone voice she remembered from their brief exchange in the back streets of Tanglehaven.

Jade held her tongue, unsure what to say, thinking carefully about what she would need to do to get out of this alive.

"She's awake," the moleman said in a raised voice, whilst keeping his eyes firmly fixed on her, indifferent to her lack of response.

Jade's last hope of the situation being resolved quickly or painlessly, at least as far as she was concerned, slipped away. The sight of the moleman with the only weapon that could harm her in his hand did little to improve her outlook on what the next few moments might hold for her. Then there was the fact that an experienced solider was comfortable talking in a raised voice, which meant it was highly likely they were quite some distance from anyone who might be bothered by a little noise. In all likelihood they were very deep in the woods now, far away from the city. She briefly wondered how they had managed to move so quickly with her unconscious body, and the wounded woman, until it dawned on her that the barmaid was probably not wounded at all. That meant that between the four of them, and the donkey, moving her around had probably not been particularly troublesome. Then she remembered the blue light. The blow it struck her

136

as it engulfed her, strangely at odds with the warmth it seemed to cocoon her in. It was like being hit by a thick, fluffy concrete pillow. What the hell had that been? And in that moment, she realised just how badly she had underestimated the party. She savoured the irony. Just as she relied on the perceived frailty of her human form to deliver a killing blow, so it dawned on her that they had done the same thing to her.

She smiled a great big smile. She threw her head back and laughed hard and long. If you can't beat them, she thought.

"Afternoon," she blurted out in the cheeriest voice she could muster. "I believe we've met before, but not been formally introduced."

It was the moleman's turn to be silent. He had met one or two demons in his time and had mixed feelings about them. On one hand they were relatively honest, pragmatic, and straightforward; all attributes he highly valued. He considered them, in a roundabout sort of a way, trustworthy, in the sense that they were predictable. They weren't evil, per se, but they had no respect for any life other than their own, and a moral compass that only ever pointed towards themselves. Their priority in any situation was always to get as much of anything that took their fancy as possible, and they would do anything to ensure they did not have to return to the Abyss. The Abyss, a prison more than a home, was where demons who found themselves on the wrong end of a runeblade went.

Chag did not think much of their conversation either, although he knew he was not the right person to be making judgments when it came to general affability and small talk. He grunted at her in response, before walking away to join the rest of the group who sat a few feet away around a fire munching on their dinner.

The night passed very slowly for Jade. For much of it she watched them talking. There was a lot of talking, and though she couldn't hear every word, it became clear that they hadn't yet decided what they were going to do with her. As the conversations wore on, she found herself wishing someone would do something, if only to break the boredom. Eventually, in a bid to not be ignored, she yelled out across the clearing, "Hey, anyone want to talk to me? Or stab me?"

There was an abrupt silence around the fire. One by one, the group turned to look at her.

"I was just wondering if you wanted to ask me any questions. I mean, you've gone to quite the effort to get me here after all," Jade continued.

There was muttering between the group and to her surprise, the barmaid stood up. As she had guessed, the woman had been faking everything. Her left hand was free of its bandages and her face restored to its usual rosy-cheeked glory.

The woman walked towards her and immediately Jade sensed a change in the atmosphere within the clearing. It had suddenly become very close, uncomfortable, even violent. There was something oddly familiar about the feeling. It was old, very old.

As the woman got closer, Jade noticed something wasn't quite right about her. It had nothing to do with her sudden ownership of the situation. It had nothing to do with the confidence or purposefulness in her step. It was something more subtle. There were inconsistencies that she couldn't quite put her finger on.

As the woman moved away from the light of the fire that flickered, casting shadows about the clearing, her face seemed to contort. At first Jade thought it might just be the shadows dancing around the trees, but the closer the woman got, the more apparent it became that it was not shadows changing their shape, but the woman's face. At first the changes were subtle, but the closer she came, the greater the shift, as features melted away or exploded outwards. Eyes grew where eyes should not have been, at least not on a human face, and her skin became mottled, then scales protruded momentarily before being shed. And somewhere behind the movement, visible through fine cracks that sometimes bled, was a fierce blue light.

"And what questions do you want to answer?" Darl asked, her voice surprisingly cold and her manner curt. Jade kicked her legs, attempting to scrabble away from whatever it was that was coming towards her. Things had certainly got a bit more interesting, but this was absolutely the wrong kind of interesting.

"Ones about whatever you want to know," Jade stuttered, her heart thumping in her chest. "I obviously have something you want or want to know, so just ask me."

"Why should I trust your answers?" the woman asked, now so close to Jade she could feel her breath on her face. At least Jade thought she should be able to feel the woman's breath on her face, but she wasn't sure that she could. Jade froze as her mind went to war with itself over what it thought she should have been feeling and seeing, and what she actually felt and saw.

Details, Jade thought to herself, grab the details, the tiny things that don't change. Hold on to them. Jade had encountered creatures on her travels who changed shape to deceive and destroy their prey. She had long ago learnt the secret to surviving their deception was to find the little things about them that didn't change. Eye colour, teeth, a scent. Find that consistency, that certainty and hold onto it, because it was the essence of their being and once you had their essence you had a target.

"Why shouldn't you trust me?" Jade stammered, scanning the woman's face, searching for something, anything that wasn't changing or melting or twisting. But nothing stayed the same; everything moved and melted and reformed. And then it stopped. A pair of sparkling emerald eyes were suddenly nestling on either side of an absent nose demanding Jade return their hungry gaze, and as she stared back, the rest of the face melted to the darkest black, absent not only of colour and light, but also of existence. Jade swore she was now staring into the nothing, the bottom of the Void, and the only thing holding her back from falling eternally through all that nothing were those grasping, soul-thirsty eyes. The stare went on and on. And then the eyes fell, dropping back and down, until they were distant burning pin pricks of eldritch light nestled in the dark sockets of a broken skull.

"By the angels. Who are you?" Jade screamed, losing what was left of the control she had been frantically trying to hold onto. She wriggled and writhed against the tree, desperate to be anywhere but in front of that face and those eyes.

The eyes bored into her mind. She could feel them stalking through it. Sharp talons ripped shrouds from her darkest secrets and sliced through the seals on her most private thoughts. She felt a million, cold, lifeless fingers jabbing into her head. The pin prick eyes stared at her and a thin, cracked voice sang over and over, "I know all your secrets."

"No. No! Make it stop!" Jade yelled. "Make it stop, make it stop, make it stooooopppp!"

It stopped.

Fear is an emotion demons know well. They cause it, they use it, but they seldom succumb to it. Jade now knew for the first time in her existence what it felt like to be wrapped up in it, and she had no desire to experience it a second time. Finding herself able to close her eyes once again, she blinked. As her eyelids raised, the woman appeared further away now, more human, but the inconsistencies remained. Cracks ran through her discoloured flesh, that now looked more like a patchwork of dead faces stitched together to create a mask to hide the monster that lurked below. The more she stared, the more she realised she recognised each rotting patch.

"We've told her all your secrets," a hundred whining voices sang.

"I'll talk. I'll tell you anything," Jade gasped, breathing heavily, every muscle taught.

"Promise you won't lie?" the thin, cracked, breathless voice asked from the woman's general direction. "Because you know I'll know."

Jade shuddered. "Yeah, I get it, you're really scary. What do you want to know?"

"Tell me about the Rose of Amzharr?" the voice asked.

"I don't know much about it. Just some old stories. It's a... it's a rose, and apparently it gives people eternal life or something, and you've got it," Jade snapped out her response, hoping that speed would make up for a complete lack of knowledge.

"Yes, yes," the voice replied. "Yes, you think that. But no, we don't. Now, tell me who you work for?"

"Can't," Jade replied.

"It does seem to appear that is the case," the voice said. "Poor little dear doesn't know why she's here."

"She's scared," the hundred voices whined. "She's scared because the rose is the rose. She helped it escape. She helped it escape."

"I didn't," Jade shouted back.

"She did, she did," they whined.

Jade forced her story out in a vain attempt to silence the voices. She explained about the job she had taken that had initially brought her into contact with Gerald. She explained about how she had realised he was immortal, and how she had been forced to change her plans. She explained everything she had done up until the point she had swooped down into the wall of blue light and woken to see the moleman holding her runeblade in front of her.

"Correct," the voice continued. "Why haven't you killed the lad yet?"

"Because... because..." She reached around for a reason, but for the first time she didn't have an answer to hand. Why hadn't she killed him?

"That's not an answer," the voice said, and the eyes moved closer. "Answer."

"Because... I wasn't sure it was the right thing to do," Jade spat out without thinking.

There was silence. The darkness of the night had descended. The thick canopy of the forest stopped the moon's light from entering and now Jade could see only two things, despite being able to see in the dark. Furthest away from her were the remains of the fire, mere embers that would soon die out if not tended to. Closer were the two pin-prick lights that served as the woman's eyes, once more suspended in the air, now with no sign of a face or a body to support them.

"Tell me more," the voice whispered, although now it was not quite so thin, not quite so breathless, more human.

"Okay, but you have to believe me. I thought you had the rose. I don't want the bloody rose, and frankly I'm still not sure what the hell it's got to do with anything anyway. But I'm an immortal, so I know only too well having anything to do with that thing brings a whole load of trouble with it, and if you've learnt anything about me from prodding around in my brain, you know I like to do my job, keep my head down and stay as far away from trouble as I possibly can," Jade gabbled, and in a moment of honesty that surprised even her said, "I guess when I heard mention of the rose it made me think back to the slaughter of the nymphs. That bloody flower is as good as a death sentence to immortals when it's in the hands of mortals. I needed to know what you lot were up to."

The woman stood before her once more, and an unfathomable look played across her face. Now there were no eldritch lights, no inconsistencies. She stared at the demon in a way that Jade did not quite know how to interpret. The malice was gone, and an inquisitive, maybe even thoughtful expression rested in its place.

As soon as the woman had removed herself from Jade's head the demon was overcome by exhaustion, and a sense of relief at being freed from the woman's mental predations. She had felt no pain, but her violation had left her feeling vulnerable and exposed. It was something she had never experienced before to such a degree, and whilst she had no idea of how much knowledge the woman had stolen from her, which of her secrets were no longer only hers, she felt weaker for it. Jade knew that physically the woman was no match for her, but the woman clearly had an immense strength that surpassed the need to resort to the primitive bludgeoning of her enemies. She had gone easy on Jade, and Jade knew it.

"You should probably get some rest," Jade heard the woman say, before she walked away towards the dying fire, the moleman following slightly behind her. Jade started to feel sick.

141

Chapter 18

The fire was almost dead when Darl returned to it. She slumped down on a tree trunk that Gerald and Chag had rolled up earlier in the day to serve as a seat. Chag stood a little way behind her, occasionally glancing over at Jade.

Darl was mentally and physically exhausted from her interrogation of the demon. Her emotions ran wild as she tried to process the horrors that resided in Jade's memories, whilst simultaneously trying to satiate the guilt she felt for using the power she had with the sole intention of hurting another. At some point her long auburn locks had come loose, and as she let her head fall forward her hair covered her face, shutting out a world she was too ashamed to be seen by in that moment. Without looking at what she was doing, she picked up a stick and prodded it in the direction of the fire.

After a couple of minutes flames appeared once more amongst the embers, and she felt the silence. It was a heavy, uncomfortable silence that filled the clearing and exerted so much pressure it stopped everyone in the party from talking, even Joggle. It was a silence that Darl wasn't ready for, but she understood exactly why it was there.

Not once in all the time that they had known her had Darl ever laid so much as a finger on another person, and whilst her acquaintances with Gerald and Joggle were in their infancy, her friendship with Chag extended over many decades. She had always been the voice of calm and reason in every conversation. Her mere presence relaxed people and brought them back from the brink of conflict. She could make drinking buddies of ancient enemies. But the fires of hurt and anger burn in everyone. So great was their tragedy that for nymphs those fires burnt brighter than most, and their nature meant they buried them so much deeper. So deep that few ever saw the fire, but Darl knew it was there. And really everyone else did too - deep down in that part of their soul that knew it would rain as soon as they put their washing out to dry, or told them their keys were in the house immediately after they'd locked the front door from the outside. They knew in that old part of their soul that instinctively knew when to be scared; and when to be so scared that they should act exactly as they knew, deep down, the scariest monster in the room wanted them to act, because otherwise the monster would get upset. And they knew they didn't want that to happen.

Darl looked up, and then around, unwilling to succumb to the silence. Joggle sat as still as a statue, nut in hand. Gerald's face was white with fear, paler than when she had pulled him from the clutches of the dreamwalker. Their eyes met briefly before darting away from each other, his in terror, hers in shame.

"That's better," Darl said meekly, making a show of warming her hands around the rejuvenated flames, doing her best to start a conversation that she hoped would somehow creep around the sides of the elephant in the clearing.

"What just happened?" Gerald asked nervously.

"An exchange of information," Darl replied in the most matter-of-fact voice she could muster.

"Didn't sound like an exchange. It sounded a bit more one-sided," Gerald mumbled.

"It was a lot less messy than the sort of exchange Chag would have offered," Darl replied dryly.

Gerald managed a weak smile before looking across at Chag. The moleman stood motionless, still watching Jade. "So, what did you learn from all that?" Gerald asked.

"That she knows less than we do," Darl responded, deflated. "She was hired to kill you at the time of the theft, and she was behind the massacre at the brothel. She also set the dark wolves on us. Right now, though, she's a lot more interested in what we're up to than she is in killing you. She had no idea that you had been hired to steal the rose, but she's worked it out now. So, like any immortal would be when the rose is involved, she's nervous in case she gets implicated in the theft and suspicious about whoever it was who hired her. Fulfilling that contract couldn't be further from her mind for now."

"Who hired her then?" Gerald asked.

"No idea," Darl replied, with a shake of her head. "She doesn't know, and her memory is so awash with blood and pain I couldn't bring myself to see if there was an image of whoever did pay for her services in there somewhere. If there is a memory of her meeting them, it's buried deep, and I don't have the stomach to go digging for it."

"And the dreamwalker?" Gerald asked hopefully. "What does she know about that?"

Darl took a deep breath before replying, "Nothing."

143

"You expect me to believe that she's only following us because she thinks we're interesting?" Gerald snarled, angry that once again their best efforts appeared to have ended in yet another dead end. "Does she really not have any more of a plan than following us around for a bit?"

"No," Darl replied. "She's still trying to work out what to do. The only thing she's certain about is that the rose has to find its way back to Death, and however that happens it has to make her look good."

"Does that mean she's technically on our side?" Joggle asked, taken back by Darl's revelation. Gerald scowled at his interpretation of the situation.

"Not at the moment, like I said, she thinks we have it. If she knew otherwise, well, I suppose she would consider helping us," Darl replied.

"By the angels, what are you suggesting?" Gerald spat, "Inviting that fiend to join us."

"You'd be able to keep an eye on her," Chag interjected, briefly returning his gaze to the group.

"If we killed her, we wouldn't need to do either," Gerald raged, his anger bubbling over. "This is getting ridiculous. We run around like idiots banging our heads repeatedly against brick walls trying to convince ourselves we're making progress. And all that really seems to be happening is we're finding more people who want to kill me."

"Surely, she can't be trusted?" Joggle chipped in, hoping that either Darl or Chag would reconsider what they seemed to be suggesting.

"If Death doesn't have the rose and we have to go out and find it, she would certainly consider being part of the effort to get it back advantageous," came Darl's lacklustre response.

"That's a very roundabout way of not saying yes," Joggle scolded, folding his arms and raising an eyebrow.

"No. No. No. No way," Gerald shouted. "That's it. I've had it. I'm done with all this scary flower nonsense. As far I can see it clearly doesn't matter who has it. Let's face it, it's been seventy odd years since I stole the thing and there hasn't been an apocalypse. The world seems to be pretty much as rubbish as it's always been, and the only person anyone seems to want to kill is me. So, since I clearly won't be missed if I do die, it seems the only logical way to end this is for us all to pack up and go home. Whoever wants to kill me can, and then all this nonsense can be forgotten about again."

Darl exploded with rage at Gerald's words. Her human shell disintegrated, blue flames erupted from her limbs, and she threw herself at him, knocking him off the tree trunk he sat on and pinning him to the ground. "Thousands of my kind were slaughtered so a mere handful of your kind could live beyond their allotted time, all because of that bloody rose. Do you understand what it's like to have your friends and relatives butchered for the benefit of irrelevant mortals? I know, and I will not have it happen again. The last time my people cowered away, too scared to defend themselves, hoping that someone would do something to help us. Mortals and immortals failed to lift even a finger until we were almost wiped from the world, and then they only helped because they had watched our suffering and feared that they might be next. I've lived long enough to put away the unhelpful grudges I once held against everyone and everything that watched and did nothing. I will not be an idle coward again, because to do nothing would make me the same as all those who did nothing to help my people until it was too late.

"I don't know where the rose is, but it should have been shielded from the mortals, and yet someone commissioned you to take it. And someone else commissioned her to kill you after you had taken it. That means at least two other people know about it. So, you will excuse me if I feel the need to know exactly where that wicked plant is. And if you want to walk away, fine. The next time one of your dreams results in you flooding your bed linen with your own blood, I will take great comfort in knowing that you were happy to accept that fate."

When she had finished speaking, she held his gaze a few seconds longer. White hot anger coursed through her. She felt so disappointed that he, of all people, was questioning her, belittling her. She resisted the urge to punch him, because she knew if she did not, that punch would only be the first, and she could not promise that there would ever be a last. She sprang to her feet and ran into the forest.

There was silence in the clearing. Gerald lay in the mud. Joggle stared off in the direction Darl had rushed away in, and Chag shook his head before turning to walk slowly over to where Jade sat.

As he got closer to the demon, he could see she was awake. "Wow, didn't think I'd be glad to be sat over here tonight," Jade said groggily.

"True enough," Chag nodded in agreement, all the while keeping a steely gaze on the demon. "Been a few years since someone's upset her quite that much, present company excepted."

"I've been told I have that effect on people," Jade replied, managing a lacklustre smile.

"You know we don't have the rose," Chag said.

"I was starting to come to that conclusion," Jade replied. "She's a nymph, isn't she?"

"Last of her kind by my reckoning," Chag answered.

"You know this whole rose situation changes everything for me. It pretty much voids the contract on the lad. And I would help you to look for it," Jade said in a low tone. "If you ask nicely."

"I'd say that too if I were in your position," Chag replied quietly before turning and looking off into the night.

Chapter 19

The morning brought rain. It fell straight down onto the leafy branches high up in the tree Jade was bound to. The tree protected her from much of the downpour. However, immediately above her head, rainwater collected on a particularly large leaf until a critical weight was reached, whereupon the leaf would bend, sending a single large drop splashing onto her head before flicking back into place and beginning to collect water again.

When the water landed, it broke into little beads and balls that rolled down and around the furrows and bony ridges that jutted from her head, acting as a kind of gutter that directed most of the water down her short, stubby nose. Jade tried to catch the drops, as they dripped from the end of her nose, with her tongue. She wasn't thirsty; it simply passed the time.

The events of the previous evening had created uncertainty in the camp. Despite her best attempts to engage Chag with her sparkling conversation throughout the night the moleman's thoughts had clearly been elsewhere. He had done his best to split his attention equally between Jade, Gerald, Joggle and Darl's disappearance, but for the most part duty won out, and he spent the majority of the night silently guarding Jade.

As the sun started to rise, Gerald and the irk had started to gather their things. Chag left the demon and walked over to the firepit where they were packing, expecting them to have decided to return to the city. He was pleasantly surprised, although he didn't show it, to find that they had decided to set out to find Darl, however unrealistic that goal was.

"I wouldn't if I were you," he advised. "You know full well she's a forest spirit. This is her part of the world. She won't let anyone find her until she's good and ready. The only thing you two are going to achieve blundering around in the undergrowth out here is getting yourselves lost. And that's the best-case scenario."

"What's the worst-case scenario?" Joggle inquired.

"Lost and then eaten," Chag replied.

The pair stopped packing and stood in silence staring at the moleman.

"So, what's the plan?" Gerald asked eventually, still covered head to toe in mud from the previous night's tumble. "Surely, we're not just going to sit around here doing nothing until Darl decides to return. Isn't there something more useful we could be doing with our time?"

"Breakfast?" Jade shouted across the clearing.

"Shut up, you," Chag barked, before turning to look at her. "The one thing I don't need in this forest is another clown who talks more than they should. Keep quiet, or I'll send you and your oh-so-witty comments back to the Abyss."

Joggle clamped a paw over his mouth to stifle his support for Jade's suggestion.

"Not much we can do," Chag continued, turning back to Gerald. "This is her world, and she can go where she pleases. She won't be found unless she's wants to be. And if she does want to see any of us again, well, she'll find us."

"I'm sorry," Gerald said to Chag, looking him in the eye. "I really am."

"I believe you, boy, but sorry doesn't undo the doings. No, the best thing we can do right now is wait. See if she comes back," Chag replied, turning back to face Jade. "And as much as I'm loathe to agree with the idiot under the tree, breakfast is probably the best use of our time right now."

Gerald and Joggle didn't even bother trying to prepare a fire. The excitement of the day before had distracted them from building a shelter, and so the rain that morning had soaked everything. They simply unpacked rations of bread and ham that they had procured the previous day, in the hope that if everything went according to plan, they would be waking up somewhere in the forest with a demon tied to a tree.

Jade coughed loudly. "Excuse me, what about yours truly?" she asked.

"What about you?" Gerald shouted back angrily, without so much as a glance in her direction. He'd had very little to do with her since her capture, and the events of last night were still fresh in his mind. He had felt good about the plan to get her. However, he had not given any thought as to how it would feel to be in her presence and look her in the eyes. But even if he had, he would not have been able to imagine the intensity of the feelings that now bubbled away inside him.

The day before, as she had been slumped unconscious against the tree, he had done his best to ignore her. It had been so much easier when she hadn't been able to talk. However, the revelations of the evening had kickstarted an inferno of feelings, an unhealthy mixture of fear and anger that had exploded at the suggestion that she might join the party. Hearing her casually demanding food brought those emotions to the surface again. It ignited a fuse that led to a part of Gerald that he was only just starting to realise existed.

148

He stood up and walked slowly towards her. Chag had told Gerald that he was not to go near Jade, but that was yesterday, and today everything was different. Anyway, he figured that if the moleman still had concerns he would quickly make them known and Gerald would be called back to the damp firepit to sit on a naughty log.

He was a little surprised when Chag didn't call him back. Part of him, the part that was absolutely terrified of the mass-murdering monster that sat in front of him, wanted the moleman to order him away from the creature. The other part kept his feet moving towards her.

The closer he got the more he began to feel Jade's gaze on him. Her head was cocked to one side, and she looked intrigued more than anything. In her real form and awake she looked scary, not like she had in her human form. Gerald wondered if he would have agreed so readily to capturing her if he had seen her like this.

"Why do you think I would want to feed you?" he asked in revulsion.

"It's a good thing to do. And you're the good guys. Right?" Jade replied cheekily.

"How dare you ask me for food like I'm a servant! You tried to kill me. You killed all those people, and you left me in that room surrounded by blood and gore... and death!" Gerald spat.

"You burnt a village down, and an inn, and stole an ancient relic soaked in the blood of mortals and immortals. I'm also going to go out on a limb and suggest you might have stolen a donkey?" Jade taunted. "So, what's your point?"

Gerald opened his mouth to respond. He closed it again as he realised all he had to say was something along the lines of "your things are worse than my things". Frustration, fear, and Jade's irritatingly smug smile burnt away inside of him. The spark reached the keg.

"Murderer!" Gerald cried, anger exploding inside of him. "Murderer!"

He grabbed a thick branch from the floor and held it with both hands at one end, the other end over his shoulder, and ran at Jade. As soon as he was close enough, he swung it with every ounce of his strength and let it smash into her face. There was a sickening crack as her nose broke and black blood started to run from skin that had split around her eyebrows. He drew the branch back and swung again and again, each blow thudding into Jade's head, breaking bones and distorting her features until there was only black pulp on top of green shoulders.

Joggle watched in horror as Gerald raised the branch ready for another blow. "Aren't you going to stop that?" he asked Chag nervously.

"Nope," Chag said. "The lad has some things he needs to work through, and if Jade is sensible, she'll let him. Especially if she wants to tag along with our little bunch of forever friends."

"What?" stuttered Joggle, already in a state of shock at the violence that was pouring out of Gerald, now made worse by the thought of the demon joining them. "Setting aside the fact that both you and Darl seem to be considering letting this mass murderer join our ranks, if you don't stop him now, there isn't going to be anything of her left to join us."

"She's a demon," Chag said dismissively.

"And?" Joggle screeched, in a panicked attempt to articulate to Chag that his response was not the detailed explanation required at that moment.

"Have you not learnt anything about demons over the years?" Chag asked.

There was a pause. Joggle's eyes darted left and right, and his mouth scrunched up. "Ermmm, no."

"Wow... I'll be..." Chag said in a tone that hinted at mild shock. He took a puff of the pipe he had lit as Gerald had approached Jade. He savoured the moment of a silent irk who had just had to admit to not knowing something. Surely, he thought, this must be a world first. He continued, "Demons are shapeshifters, and they don't feel pain in the traditional sense. They certainly can't be hurt or killed with a stick."

"Well, excuse me, but that looks pretty damn painful," Joggle replied, pointing at the headless body slumped against the tree with Gerald collapsed in a heap beside it in a flood of tears.

"Don't worry, it's not what it looks like," Chag said reassuringly.

"So, what is it then?" Joggle asked. "Tell me. And please don't spare me the details."

"Empathetic magic," Chag said.

"Which is?" Joggle asked, a tinge of frustration in his voice.

"You sure do like to know everything about everything," Chag sighed. "Okay, I'm no expert, but I'll do my best to explain. It's magic that lets people see what they think they should see. Darl basically lives her life wrapped in it,"

"What?" Joggle replied, trying to process the bloody mess and the crying lad, whilst coaxing an explanation from Chag, not altogether sure which was the most difficult.

150

"Let me give you an example. Stab a demon and nothing happens. There's no blood, as such, to run anywhere and the flesh just sort of moves around a bit to accommodate the blade. That's great if you're a demon, but kind of irritating if you're trying to hurt one. It really annoys people and gets them thinking about how they can hurt them. Then it just becomes a matter of time until they figure out a way, which is not great for demons. So, to avoid people spending too much time thinking about how to hurt them, demons, and quite a lot of other minor immortals come to think about it, combine a little bit of their shapeshifting knowhow with a little bit of their magic, and essentially shapeshift into whatever the person hurting them thinks they should look like when they're being hurt," Chag explained. "It's one of those win-win situations. Eventually, the person that wants to hurt them thinks they have and stops trying, like now, and the demon gets the advantage of surprise when they decide to take their turn at hurting their assailant back. And then there's this rather specific situation. How do you think the lad would feel if Jade was sat there, head intact, unblemished and grinning that stupid grin she seems to have permanently plastered all over her face?"

"I guess he'd still be hammering away with that branch," Joggle replied.

"Maybe, but he'd also feel like she was making fun of him. That right there is demonic diplomacy at its finest. She might be as smug as you are talkative, but I'm a big believer in giving credit where it's due," Chag continued.

"So just for clarification… where's her head?" Joggle asked, ignoring Chag's comparison.

"On her body," Chag replied.

"Pardon?" Joggle asked in disbelief.

"Sorry, I forget most people don't spend their lives around empathetic magic. You do get used to it after a while. I assume you're seeing a bloody pulp, or a smashed-up skull - basically, whatever you think all those blows would have done had they landed on something a bit bigger than a human skull?" Joggle nodded a response. "The lad will be seeing whatever he thinks a human head should look like after his handiwork."

"And what are you seeing?" Joggle asked.

"It's hard to explain. I'm not immune to the effects, but I know when I see it, so I see something a bit between the two. I can see her concentrating on keeping the magic going, but I can also see a lot of mess. But don't worry, she's fine," Chag explained.

"Oh. Okay. That's erm, good then," Joggle said, clearly not thinking that anything about the situation was good. "Erm, about the other thing. When are you planning on telling him – before or after she does whatever she does to grow her head back?"

"What other thing?" Chag asked, quite enjoying this particular conversation.

"The thing about her maybe joining us," Joggle replied.

"Well, I don't see the point discussing it before she's decided what she wants to do. No point stirring up a load more angst. Especially if it could be avoided," Chag said. "I mean, she might not want anything to do with us after the lad's little outburst. Anyway, if she does want in, it's probably best coming from her."

"Doesn't it bother you that she set the dark wolves on us?" Joggle asked.

"That was before she knew anything about the rose. Look, the thing you have to get your head around about demons is that whilst they have no qualms about killing, they don't do it for the hell of it. Killing is only ever a means to an end for them. What they really love is a good deal, and they are absolute sticklers when it comes to drawing up contracts. In all honesty there's probably more demons who are lawyers than there are bounty hunters. Point is this, if she decides she wants to come with us to find the rose then she'll do it, and frankly I'd much rather have her where I can keep an eye on her. Much better than having her hanging about in the shadows, waiting for us to do the hard work, so she can kill us and claim all the glory."

Joggle considered the moleman's words briefly. There was an undeniable logic to what he had to say that the irk's lack of knowledge about demons made it impossible to argue against, without resorting to hearsay or hyperbole. Knowing that this was unlikely to cut much mustard with the old mercenary Joggle said no more. Then he decided that since there were so many unanswered questions the group needed to address, he may as well raise another one.

"Do you believe the rose is out in the world again?" he asked.

"I prefer to know things rather than believe them," Chag replied. "That's why I didn't think finding Death's front door and banging on it until he gives us an answer was the worst plan in the world. Although I never thought it would be the easiest either. Obviously, I'm keeping my fingers crossed it's back in its vase, or whatever he keeps something like that in.

Honestly, I'm not too old for another trek around the world, but I'm not so young that I want to do it with an axe in my hand."

"You're sticking to the original plan then?" the irk asked, slightly surprised.

"It's important to Darl, so it's important to me," Chag said. "I'll be camping here tonight and heading back to Tanglehaven tomorrow morning to start breaking down gates. Up to you lot whether you want to come along or not. I'm not bothered either way," the moleman said staring into space.

"And Darl?" Joggle asked.

"Like I said, she'll come and find me when she's ready," Chag replied. "Until then there's no reason to not carry on."

His piece said Chag walked over to where Gerald now knelt. Gerald leant heavily on his bloodied branch, tears exhausted, eyes ringed red. As he walked, he looked across at Jade's body. A haze of magic swam around her head, hiding it from anyone who did not know it was there, and he tried not to react as in the middle of the haze he swore he could see her sticking her tongue out at him.

"Feeling better lad?" Chag asked squatting down beside him.

"Yeah, I think so," he replied.

"Well, have a rest," Chag said, releasing the branch from his grasp and laying it on the floor. "Don't know much about demons, do you?"

"Think I know how to kill one," Gerald said brusquely.

"Not so sure you do," Chag replied, clamping his hand around Gerald's chin, and turning his head so he could see Jade's face gradually reappearing.

"By the blood of the angels..." Gerald growled, grabbing the branch again.

Chag dealt Gerald a heavy blow with the edge of his free hand that struck into the joint between his shoulder and chest. Gerald winced at the short, sharp shock that travelled through his body. His arm went limp, and the branch fell back to the floor. The moleman quickly stood and kicked the branch away, "No more," he said with a finality that stopped Gerald dead in his tracks.

"But..." the lad protested.

"But what?" Chag countered.

"But she..." Gerald tried.

"She got paid to do some stuff. So did you," Chag said gruffly.

"Why are you taking her side?" Gerald protested.

"Because I've been on her side, and you've been on her side," Chag retorted. "Has she tried to kill you in the last sixty odd years? And the dark wolves don't count."

"Well, no, but she was following us," said Gerald.

"Long way between following and killing, lad. Long way. If she wanted you dead now, she'd have done it," Chag turned to Jade. "Tell him, honestly, were you going to kill him in Tanglehaven?"

"Probably not," Jade shouted from her seat.

Chag growled, "You really don't know how to help yourself, do you?"

"You told me to be honest. I had no reason to kill him really, so if you two hadn't started chasing me around, we probably wouldn't have met," she smiled sweetly and made a noisy kissing sound. "But I'm so glad we did."

"But you were following us," Gerald moaned.

"Like the mole dude said, big difference between following and killing. Following means you're interesting, killing means you've got a price on your head," she winked.

"But don't I still have a price on my head from before?" Gerald asked.

"Nah, they paid me before I did the job, and didn't want any evidence I'd finished it. I see that as a customer failing in their obligations," Jade responded.

"Right, that's enough. The time for messing around is over," Chag said before Gerald could say anything else. "Jade, what are your plans?"

"So kind of you to ask," she replied. "Call me pessimistic, but I hadn't really made any beyond sitting under this tree in the rain. Do I have choices?"

"Well, you can stay here if you want. I'm sure you'll find your way out sooner or later. Alternatively, if you want to join us, I'm not going to say you're welcome, but you're no less welcome than either of these idiots. And to save you a question - yes, I'll be keeping the runeblade," Chag said.

"Even if I stay under the tree all by myself?" Jade asked.

"Yes," Chag replied flatly.

"Very well, you've convinced me. I'll come with you lot," she said, before closing her eyes, muttering a few words, flexing her muscles, and letting the ropes fall away from her. Gerald's jaw hit the ground.

"I'll be keeping an eye on you," Chag said, seemingly unphased by what had just happened.

"I have a feeling you won't be the only one," Jade shot back as Gerald glared at her angrily.

Although it was still early in the day, and there was plenty of time to return to the city, Chag had decided to stay for another night in case Darl made her way back to the camp. Despite everything that had happened in the last few hours, and their concerns about Jade, there remained a fragile bond between the group. Even in Darl's absence it prevented Gerald and Joggle from leaving Chag, and so they decided to stay with the moleman for another night, at least.

They passed the next few hours in silence building a shelter and talking amongst each other only when it was absolutely necessary. Jade's presence destroyed what little cohesion the group had left. The irk was nervous around her, and Gerald could not take his eyes off her. Jade, not unused to people staring at her, ignored him and got on with any tasks she was asked to do. She did her best to resist doing anything that might anger him any further. She wasn't worried about him attacking her again, but circumstances had changed, and she needed time to decide what she was going to do. She had also decided a new human disguise was required, and that meant undisturbed meditation, which she might get a chance at if the group was able to rest that night.

Only Chag seemed unperturbed by the situation. Occasionally he would bark out an order or make the kind of suggestion that was clearly an order, but mainly he just enjoyed the peace.

The rain came and went throughout the day, and as the daylight started to wane, the group settled into the relative dry of their new shelter and munched on the remains of their rations.

"What's the plan, boss?" Jade asked, a hint of sarcasm in her voice.

"We'll return to the city tomorrow if there's no sign of Darl," Chag replied. "Then we'll get to finding the entrance to that house. Darl can find us when she's good and ready."

Chapter 20

Gerald took the first watch that evening but spent most of his time watching Jade. The demon had said she had felt tired from the events of the last day or so and needed to rest. She sat cross-legged and bolt upright in a simple circle, drawn in the dirt. The circle served no purpose, but she felt the dramatic implications of it would probably annoy Gerald in some way, which made it worth the effort in her view. Her eyes were closed, and her chest gently rose and fell. Just after midnight Chag woke and relieved Gerald of his watch. Chag took no notice of Jade. He knew enough to know that once a demon was resting, they were unlikely to wake unless they were forced to defend themselves.

As he paced silently around the camp, he became aware of shapes in the undergrowth. His eyesight was not impeded by the dark in the same way Gerald's was. And Gerald's watch had been impeded far more by his focus on the danger he perceived to be within the camp, and so the possibility that there might be any outside of it had not even occurred to him.

Chag noticed the odd shapes immediately. In the dark, through human eyes, they would have looked like shadows nestling harmlessly in the places shadows would be expected to nestle. Through Chag's eyes they looked awkward and out of place, and their dark, sombre colours didn't quite match their surroundings, didn't blend with the shadows they aspired to look like. As he backed slowly away towards the shelter, claw reaching for the sword at his belt, a spark ignited a fire that ran in a circle around the clearing, creating a flaming barrier that burnt at roughly waist height.

The shapes unfolded. Cloaks were thrown over shoulders and crossbows were levelled. Looking around, Chag estimated that there were ten, maybe twelve of the shapes. The heat haze that hovered over the flames and the thick foliage away from the clearing obscured their number, but when you're clearly outnumbered, you're outnumbered, and exact numbers were not a priority for the moleman.

Chag assumed they were humans. They were human-shaped, but their faces were covered by rough cloth masks that prevented the look-'em-in-the-eye test Chag used to identify his enemies in situations like these. Despite their obscured faces, he felt there was probably sufficient evidence, on balance, to assume that they were up to no good. One of the group lowered their crossbow, stepped forward and spoke.

"Give us the nymph," the speaker said in a loud, clear voice.

"She's not here," Chag replied in his trademark monotone.

"Take us to her then," the voice demanded.

"Can't," Chag responded.

"Fine," the voice replied without any emotion. "Kill them. Find the nymph."

The speaker stepped back and raised their crossbow.

A scream shattered the silence as Jade, in her new human form, leapt through the air with what looked like a sword in each hand. Chag took a moment to realise that the muscular woman with short, green hair jumping from the direction of the shelter was Jade. As alter egos went, it was certainly a change from the old lady and a lot closer to her true form. Before her feet touched the ground, a blade was already buried in the leader's head and blood had showered her. Face red with gore, she flashed a smile of white teeth as the flames reflected off the sheen of the warm liquid. She looked every inch the demon she hid inside.

Her attack drew the attention of all the shapes and, perhaps most usefully for Chag, their crossbows. As she landed, she twisted to look at the moleman and shouted, "Run!", before flipping towards the closest assailant and ramming her second blade, which Chag swore for a moment was really just her hand, through their throat as they fumbled their crossbow in an attempt to aim it at the rapidly moving target.

The remaining attackers had already moved to positions where they could get a clear shot at the woman. Realising that regardless of how quickly and erratically she moved between attacks, when she struck, her movement would slow and so she would be in a roughly predictable place for at least a second or two, the attackers waited with crossbows ready as she danced towards her next victim. More ready than the previous two had been, but still far from composed, the warrior swung their crossbow wildly about in front of them with both hands, hoping to land a blow. Jade held back just long enough for the crossbow to swing past where the attacker had hoped her body would have been. She brought a blade up in a slicing motion, allowing it to cut through the fighter's wrists, sending the crossbow with their hands still attached hurtling off into the trees. Her blade reached the top of its natural arch before turning and gliding down towards their shoulder, slicing through the warrior's clavicle. As blood plumed into the air, every crossbow trigger clicked, and bolts flew towards the space Jade occupied.

Most of the bolts went wide, two slammed into the handless body as it dropped and another two stuck into Jade, one in her shoulder, one in her rib cage. She let out a scream which made Chag roll his eyes as he hustled Joggle and Gerald away from the fighting; not more amateur dramatics, he thought.

Swords were now drawn around the clearing and the flames had spread inwards towards the shelter, which was now alight. Despite the bolts that protruded from her body, Jade had managed to knock the head off another fighter, but in the process an opportune blow from another assailant had caught her across the back. The fighter watched as a gash opened and red blood started to flow. Far more worrying for Jade, though, was that the blow had knocked her off balance, making it hard for her to defend herself as she tried desperately to find a footing. The attacker, who had struck the lucky blow across her back, spotted an opening, and let their reflexes go to work. Their front foot lunged forward, and they thrust their sword towards the gap that had opened between her hip and ribs. The blade did the rest, sliding into her flesh. The force of the strike knocked her to the ground. As she fell, she wondered if Gerald would appreciate this. He bloody better had.

Gerald had awoken to the sound of the voice demanding Darl be handed over. Dragged from a deep slumber, he suddenly found himself lying there, eyes wide open, heart pounding. Joggle was still sound asleep, unaware of what was going on outside. Gerald lay frozen as the voice, unheard for nearly seventy years, spoke once again.

He forced himself to move, forced himself to quietly get out of the makeshift bed on the floor. He wondered if the voice knew he was there, and then he wondered if the owner of the voice was outside. He crept forward to see, knife in hand, and just as he was able to look into the dark beyond the fire that now surrounded the shelter, all hell broke loose. He heard Jade scream, saw someone who looked suspiciously similar to her, although admittedly a lot more human, fling herself through the air with a short sword in each hand. He saw Chag turn and run towards the shelter as Jade shouted something. Gerald grabbed Joggle and stuffed the still-sleeping irk into the first bag that came to hand. As Chag entered the shelter, he motioned he was ready to leave and together they hurried around the back, jumped through the flames, and crashed into the bushes beyond.

The forest behind the shelter was thick, but Gerald found, even in the dark, he was able to pick a path between the trees with Chag following surprisingly closely behind.

"Do you think she'll kill them all?" Gerald asked.

"Don't think that's her plan," Chag replied.

"Why not? She can survive a sodding branch to the head, swords can't be any worse," Gerald huffed as he ducked under a branch.

"When you're like her, killing a lot of people when they're all spaced out and happy to wait their turn for a fair fight is like picking daisies. But they won't be waiting their turn; they'll crowd her and overpower her. They may not be able to kill her, but we both know she can be captured, and I get the feeling Jade ain't the sort to let that happen to her again in a hurry."

"So, what's her plan?" Gerald asked.

"No idea. She's already put in the hard yards, though, giving us a chance to escape, so don't waste her effort. You just focus on getting us as far away from that lot as possible," Chag replied, closing the conversation down.

The sounds of fighting soon died in the clearing. The fighter standing over Jade's broken body raised their sword a final time and hacked her head off, before kicking it into the fire that burnt where the shelter had been. Silently the warriors reloaded their crossbows and made their way into the trees behind the shelter, disappearing as suddenly and completely as they had arrived.

Chapter 21

Jade's head reappeared on her body, the bolts were expelled from her flesh, and the blood disappeared. She sighed as she stood up, brushed the dirt from herself and did her best to inspect the damage to her clothing. She shook her head as she realised a new shirt was undoubtedly required. She wondered if the group had had any discussions about how damaged clothing should be compensated. After a brief think, she decided that the subject probably hadn't made the top of Chag's list of concerns, and the others certainly weren't professional enough to have thought about it. That was the great thing about having paying clients, she thought: you had someone to bill when your tailoring got damaged. This reminded her - there had not been any discussions about payment for her amongst the group, and for the first time it dawned on her that this adventure, if she decided to be part of it, was likely to cost her dearly. The question she now needed to answer was: what cost was she willing to bear?

She walked into the bonfire and rummaged around in the burning remains of the shelter until she found her shoulder bag. Things had become complicated, but there was an order to things. Living before the dead, she reminded herself, and fished about in her bag until she found a small mirror. She held it up and looked at herself, wondering how the transformation had gone. The interruption had cut her meditation short, so whilst the face that stared back at her wasn't exactly what she was going for, the resemblance in her new face to her own made her smile. "Cute," she said out loud. "It'll do for now."

Despite everything, she felt surprisingly good about the night's events so far. She made her way to where the body of the speaker lay. She had recognised the voice. It had hired her all those years ago to kill Gerald. It looked as though one loose end had already been addressed. She didn't want to get ahead of herself, but at this rate the rose would be back where it belonged by the end of the week, and there would definitely not be any refund requests now.

"Well, might as well see who you are," she whispered as she crouched down by the body. She was unimpressed by the speaker's choice of clothes. The body seemed to be covered head to toe in sack cloth. The cloth that covered the face was dark with blood, as would be expected. She picked up a stick from the ground and started to poke at the head, intrigued to see the face beneath the mask, but cloth gave way to reveal only more cloth. She dropped the stick and started to pull at the material, before widening her search to the rest of the body. It quickly became apparent that whatever the thing was, it was not a human. It appeared to be made of layers of blood-soaked material, shaped into human proportions using ties and bandages. Once through the outer layers, the consistency of the material changed, and she began to pull out rags and stuffing that had been crammed together to give the body some shape. She started to pull the rags apart until she found what looked like a heart. The organ was loose, unconnected to anything, dry and shrivelled, but it was definitely a heart. "Ick," she said, tossing it to one side before continuing with her search.

Moments later the bodies of all three soldiers she had killed had all been unpicked, and she sat in front of the fire with three shrivelled hearts in her hands. She began to suspect that the voice had probably not belonged to the speaker, in the traditional sense; these were obviously some sort of automata that had been controlled from some distance away. She wondered how far, and whether the actual owner of the voice knew that she was there. Why was nothing easy anymore, she thought. Bloody Gerald. Then, in that moment she made her decision - a decision, she strongly suspected, that would cost her everything and almost certainly not be worth it.

"By the angels," she smiled. "I suppose doing the right thing once every lifetime doesn't make it a habit, just the exception that proves the rule."

She wrapped the hearts up in one of the many pieces of cloth that now littered the clearing and stuffed them into her bag. Centuries of life experience told her that although she thought they were a bit weird she was bound to run into someone, sooner or later, who would have sufficient interest in them that they would be willing to trade something useful for them. Once the hearts were securely stowed, she pushed her hand into the bag a little further until she felt a small, sharp-edged crystal. She pulled it out.

The stone was blue with orange veins running through its centre. It was set in silver and attached to a thin chain. The chain had a tiny clasp which she undid before fastening it around her neck.

"Help me find Darl little stone," she said, standing up, closing her eyes and turning slowly on the spot. As she turned to face the direction Chag, and then the remaining cloth warriors, had disappeared in, she felt a burning sensation against her skin and swore. This is going to hurt, she thought.

She flexed her shoulder blades and forced her wings out through the back of her shirt. Now was not the time for subtlety nor, it would appear, modesty. Her body rearranged itself to her demon form, and the shirt fell to the ground, joining the other torn rags.

She took to the air and followed the direction of the stone, as its heat grew in intensity the closer it got to Darl. Gritting her teeth as it burnt white hot against her skin, she burst through the forest canopy, relieved that Darl's location was so far from the shelter, and so too from the cloth soldiers. As she landed, the flesh on her chest was starting to blister. She reached up and tore the necklace from her neck, breaking the thin chain and holding the stone at arm's length. She breathed heavily from the exertion of the flight, and in an attempt to manage the pain that coursed through her body. She looked out from the small group of trees she had landed in to see Darl stood in the centre of a small stone circle, blue light radiating from her. A chill ran down Jade's spine. Darl was surrounded.

Chapter 22

Gerald and Chag moved as quickly as they could. The sounds of fighting behind them had stopped. Gerald didn't know what to make of it. He hoped that it meant they had moved out of earshot of the clearing and were now far away from the warriors that had surrounded them.

Chag nudged him to move faster, which he assumed meant that whatever the silence indicated to the moleman was not as good as he had hoped. Not for the first time on the journey Gerald wished he had stayed in the sanctuary. Although he had quite enjoyed the walk to Tanglehaven, dark wolf attack aside, and exploring the city streets had built a confidence in him he hadn't felt for so many years, he was once again running for his life, and it was considerably less fun than sitting by the lake waiting to go to sleep at night. Suddenly he was finding that actions, even ones from a lifetime ago, had consequences, and he much preferred it when they hadn't.

He looked behind and saw a hooded head and set of shoulders in the gloom. The person was quite away behind them, but if their pursuer had been at the shelter, they were moving quickly. He wondered whether Jade would be able to help them again; maybe it wasn't quite so bad having the psycho demon on their side. Another nudge from Chag made him push the thought from his mind and return his focus to where he was going.

He looked behind again and now there were two figures making their way through the trees. He saw a third. They were getting much closer. Continually glancing behind and to the side, he started to misplace his footing. His right foot slid into a loop of roots, and he found himself falling. Chag grabbed him, pulled him upright and set him on his feet again.

"Don't look back, don't look to the side, just look where you're going. Get out of here! Find Darl!" Chag barked. Unable to do as he was told, Gerald glanced back to see the moleman unsheathe his sword and turn to face their pursuers.

"Run, you idiot!" he heard the moleman say.

He turned again as a clash of steel rang out in the night air. He broke into a run, only to see that more masked men were now ahead of them. Not sure what to do, he drew his knife, and in an act of desperation as much as defiance, hurled it towards one of them. There was a soft thud as the blade buried itself in the target's face and they went down. Amazed by the accuracy of the throw, Gerald threw another two knives, which Chag had given to him following the wolf attack. Another two fell, but now they were surrounded, and he found himself moving backwards towards Chag.

The moleman had dispatched the three warriors that had been closest to him, but the others that appeared weren't interested in getting any closer than they had to, which was a reasonable distance given that they all had crossbows. Neither Chag nor Gerald had the speed, or element of surprise, that Jade had to enable them to close the distance without being shot at in the process.

Silence descended as they stood wondering what would happen next. The masked men took aim and several triggers clicked as one. The bolts lurched forward and a mist shrouded Chag, Gerald, and Joggle, who was shaken but gladly removed from events in the shoulder bag.

The bolts dissolved as they passed into the mist and the ground erupted around the feet of the masked warriors. Skeletons shot from the ground clutching swords. They moved so quickly the masked soldiers barely had time to react before blades hacked into them, reducing them to nothing but bloody rags which blew away in a slight wind that stirred in the trees, littering them around the forest.

The mist and the skeletons disappeared as swiftly as they had arrived. Chag and Gerald stood, blades in their hands, confusion in their minds. In the distance a pinprick of light shone. It advanced directly towards them, passing through trees and bushes without slowing. As it got closer, it became apparent the light shone from a lantern held by an apparition that seemed to flicker in and out of existence. The apparition was of a man, his face and body swollen by plague, clothes ragged and tattered beyond any possible chance of recognition of when or where he may have lived. He reached out a hand and beckoned to the companions. They looked at each other, uncertain whether to follow.

"Do we have a choice?" asked Gerald.

"We always have a choice," Chag replied. "It just might not lead to a long, happy life."

"Yeah, that much I know," Gerald said.

"You're still alive, right?" Chag asked.

"I wouldn't mind a bit of happiness as well, though," Gerald replied.

"Can't have a happy life if you aren't living. At least you're halfway there," Chag said.

The apparition appeared to nod in agreement at the moleman's words and beckoned once more.

"Hey ho, I suppose there are worse things we could be doing right now," Gerald said with a weak laugh.

"Always," Chag replied, a broad smile lighting up his face. He might not have been young enough to enjoy the current turn of events, he thought as the apparition turned, but he was certainly old enough to appreciate them.

Chapter 23

Jade stood with her arm outstretched, the crystal pendant dangling from the chain in her hand glowed white hot. She looked through the trees at Darl. The nymph stood in the middle of a small stone circle. Opposite her was a man. He was tall and thin with a sharp face that had a healthy complexion. Everything about him was neat and ordered. He wore clothes cut in the most modern style, with white trousers tucked into brown riding boots and a dark blue jacket with black trim around the collar and cuffs. She thought she could also see the hint of a bright yellow waistcoat.

Darl's slight body was a swirling mix of oranges and purples now. She was in conversation with the man. She had not returned to her human form which Jade took to be a bad sign, especially when she considered the ranks of skeleton soldiers standing silently to either side of the pair as they conversed. For a second the man raised his hand as if pausing the conversation. He turned his head and without any hesitation or uncertainty looked Jade in the eye, a considerable feat given they were separated by a couple of hundred metres. The demon froze. The man lowered his hand and his gaze returned to Darl. Their conversation continued.

Jade watched, for the second time in her life genuinely terrified and completely unsure as to what her next move should be. Out of the corner of her eye she saw a lantern light floating up the hill, held high in the hand of a plague-ridden apparition. Behind the apparition walked Chag and Gerald. She noticed no skeletons accompanied them. They walked at an easy pace towards the circle, passing unhindered by the ranks of undead without any hesitation. Darl saw them and ran to Chag, reaching out and folding him in an embrace. As soon as they separated, Darl turned to Gerald and they also hugged, not as dramatically, but the embrace looked comfortable and lingered beyond politeness. Darl's body language seemed more controlled, less familiar, but there was an undeniably deep blue glow within her which gave Jade pause for thought.

The apparition slowly faded and the three made their way back to the ring of stones. The smartly dressed man ushered them in as though it were a room rather than a circle of eight worn rocks, that stood no higher than Chag's knees.

"You too," a voice whispered in Jade's ear. "That's your decision. Isn't it?"

Jade's breathing faltered. She didn't feel compelled to join the group in the circle. Flight in both senses of the word was still a possibility, and she knew it would have been easy. But the voice was right. It was her decision. She had made a choice. It was a strange feeling.

For centuries, millennia even, she had clung to the shadows, existed alone, hunted, and killed for mortals and immortals she had despised. She had convinced herself that her actions were an inevitability. Afterall, the lives she had taken were on the orders of others. They would have been taken by someone; why not her? A job was a job, and it paid well. It was for this reason she had always considered herself a tool, an instrument wielded by those who wished to shape the world as they chose.

She reflected on this as she made her way towards the stone circle. As she got closer to it, she started to feel its energy. It fizzed and crackled as she approached. The stones might have been small, but they were old and still had much of their power. She noticed that all eyes were on her as she walked, including those of the irk who had made his way out of the bag and was now sitting on Gerald's shoulder.

"Told you, lad," Chag said quietly to Gerald. "It doesn't always pay to let people know just how tough you really are."

Darl looked over at Chag, a streak of orange light flashing through her. "She's saved more of us than she's killed," Chag replied. "In my mercenary days it would have got her a seat at the table."

The man ushered Jade into the circle. She felt the energy temporarily recede, as she stepped between two of the rocks.

"I suppose now we're all here, introductions are customary," the man's voice was exactly as his clothing suggested, clipped, elegant and confident.

There are those whose presentation to the world marks them out as rich or powerful. His presentation went far beyond either of those. Something about him marked him out as a singularity within the universe, a constant, one of the very pillars of existence even.

"My name is Hobb," he said. "Others know me as Death, but that is a name for another day."

A respectful silence enveloped the group. Even Jade stood quietly, eyes cast towards the floor.

"It has come to my attention that you have been seeking an audience with me, and recent events have made it necessary that I seek one with you," he continued. "I think you are all aware that some seventy years ago this gentleman removed a certain piece from my collection of antiquities. I have spent quite some time searching for it, but despite my best efforts, it appears to have slipped far beyond my reach, and so I thought, who better to return it than the man who stole it?"

Gerald found himself face to face with Hobb and he felt as though they stood alone. Hobb's stare penetrated to the core of his being and in a second Gerald knew that it was Hobb, and not the rose, that had extended his life.

"Why?" Gerald just about managed to squeeze out.

"Because you intrigued me. It's not every day of the week that someone successfully relieves me of a part of my collection. In my experience it is wise to keep that which you do not fully understand available, so to speak, because until you properly understand it, you don't really know whether it presents a threat or is simply a little... misguided," Hobb explained calmly. "I learnt that lesson the first time I let someone take the rose from me."

"So, am I an immortal now?" Gerald managed to force out.

"For now," Hobb replied.

Gerald went to ask another question, only to find his voice gone. Hobb raised his hand. "No more. You owe me the rose you took from me. I owe you nothing. Consider what I have told you a gesture of good will on my part."

Hobb stepped back from Gerald and the atmosphere in the bubble seemed to ease. "I believe you all know the story of the prince of the Lost Lands who was said to have organised the theft of the rose. There is sadly more truth to this story than one would wish. Yes, there was a prince and a peasant. Yes, they and their families are all now beyond the veil, but it was not the prince who commissioned the theft; he was merely a very convincing distraction, which I fell for. I have cast my agents around the world in a bid to seek the rose out, yet whoever has it has managed to elude me. However, it seems the current keeper has decided the time is ripe for them to sneak back into the world. They must not be allowed to sneak very far."

"Do you know who it is?" Darl asked.

"Sadly no, but the rose is a parasite. It claims a host, so to some degree the who is irrelevant. I have heard reports that the creations that stalked you tonight are being seen frequently in the Lost Lands. They are raiding, although so far it is not clear to what purpose, or on whose behalf. The last time I saw such creatures, though, they were commanded by the sorceress who stole the rose. So, I would suggest, Gerald, this is where you begin your search," Hobb continued.

"And what about the rest of us?" Darl asked.

"Darl, of all the group you have the very least obligation to me. You are, I understand, the last of your kind and I would not push a species to extinction in the pursuit of the very thing that caused their downfall," he looked in turn at each of the others. "You also have no obligation to be here. As I whispered in each of your ears, you have your own decisions to make."

"The world is not a museum, and you are not its curator," Darl said firmly, but respectfully. "I will speak for my race, and the nymphs will no longer let our fate be decided by old oaths that should have been retired centuries ago."

"I'm game," Jade said, momentarily at peace with the idea that the first big decision she had made in her life might also be her last.

"I guess that just leaves you," Chag said, looking up at Joggle as he chewed on a nut.

"I happen to know that the Lost Lands are very beautiful at this time of year - well, as beautiful as anywhere can be without a shred of vegetation. A visit would be most enjoyable," Joggle replied, chest puffed out.

"What about you?" Darl asked Chag.

"Of course, I'm coming with you. Where else would I go?" Chag replied in a voice rich in sincerity, but devoid of any enthusiasm.

"That's not the reason to do this," Darl replied. "I know you laid your weapons to rest a long time ago. It's too much for me to ask you to come with us just because you think you should for my sake."

Chag's silent response told her everything she already knew.

"You don't need to make any decisions now," she said, and swore she heard a short sigh of relief escape the moleman's mouth.

"An interesting party if ever I have seen one," Hobb said as skeletons faded from existence outside the stones. "Very well. I shall make travel arrangements for you on the Void ships in the coming days. Until then, find somewhere to rest. And please stay out of trouble."

"How do we know that there won't be more of those things coming after us?" Jade asked.

"You don't, but I will do my best to keep you hidden from prying eyes, and protected, for as long as possible," Hobb reassured them. "But you must be ready to leave as soon as your ship is ready."

With that Hobb vanished and the group found themselves alone once again in the forest. There was a stillness. The morning sun broke through the leaves and dappled the ground. For the briefest moment, the scent of summer jasmin laced the air.

"What now?" Gerald asked.

"We walk," said Chag with a smile.

Chapter 24

Back in the city, Jade led them to the abandoned warehouse she had stayed in. Although it lacked the comforts of the inn, it was warm and dry, which even Joggle had to admit was an improvement on the shelter in the woods. They spent the next few days resting, wondering what the future held. Jade's acceptance into the group was far from immediate. She might have bought time for Chag, Gerald, and Joggle to escape but, with the exception of Chag, the others were nervous of the violence she was capable of, and no one felt they understood or trusted her reasons for joining them. Chag was the most sympathetic to her decision, but he was far too wrapped up in spending what time he could with Darl to make any attempt to help Jade integrate with the others. He had not actually made a choice on the hill, but as each day passed it became clear which direction he intended to take. Gerald had noticed their experience in the woods had aged Chag visibly. He seemed slower, grumpier, and less forgiving on the odd occasion he would call Gerald over, put a sword in his hand and teach him how to use it. So, it came as no surprise when a messenger arrived at the door from Hobb with documents of passage for a Void ship that only four names were listed.

Before they left the warehouse on the day they were due to travel, Chag gave Darl a long hug goodbye before wishing the party luck and excusing himself. He had found work in a local bar and did not want to be late for his first shift.

The group made their way by foot to the docks. Gerald was only too happy for Darl and Jade to lead the way. Although it was his task to return the rose, he felt once again that he was out of his depth, and so clung to any opportunity to hide in the shadows of those he considered far more able than himself.

Since the events in the forest, Joggle had taken to traveling in his shoulder bag. Gerald found something oddly reassuring that at least one person in the group looked to him for help, although he suspected the irk's travel choices were mainly driven by laziness, and that Joggle knew Gerald would be the last person to complain.

It was fair to say that Darl and Jade had reached an uneasy accord during the days they spent together, and a mutual understanding was in the early stages of growth. They had started to find some subjects of shared interest and spoke civilly to one another when it was necessary. There was, however, one thing that did manage to bond all four together equally in excitement and fascination, although they showed it in varying ways, which was the anticipation of the journey through the Void.

The Void flowed between the seas and oceans of the world. Mostly it was something seagoing vessels had to navigate around, extending most journeys between lands by weeks, or even months. The exception to this was the Lost Lands. The continent had been isolated by the Void in the early days, when its rulers had stripped it of any vegetation that would allow the oversight of the land by the Guardians. That meant that, other than in the most exceptional circumstances, it was only possible to reach it by sailing directly through the Void. The Void was a grey mist that constantly fluctuated in thickness. In parts it was little more than a light fog; elsewhere it had the consistency of water, and sometimes even land. Consequently, the only way to safely cross it was in small boats piloted by wizards. It was an expensive way to travel and not a journey many people would ever undertake. On the day they were due to travel they made their way, by foot, to the docks. They were all dressed for the occasion, resplendent in new clothes fetched from Hobb's personal tailors that very morning. Even Joggle had donned a tiny velvet waistcoat in the spirit of the next stage of their journey.

They smiled as they heard the bustle of the busy port get closer. Darl pushed the sadness that Chag would no longer be at her side from her mind and glanced around at her new companions. For the second time since meeting Gerald, she was embarking on a journey with only the faintest notion of what had to be done, and where they were going. For the life of her she could not understand why Joggle had decided to come, but she knew that his race had suffered as needlessly as her own when the witch had first hunted the lesser immortals in her quest for longevity. And then there was Jade, the hunter, the murderer, the mercenary, but above all the unknown. Darl slipped a hand inside the fold of her skirts to tap the hilt of the runeblade Chag had given her that morning.

"I guess you can't run a bar without breaking the odd bottle," she said to herself.

Printed in Great Britain
by Amazon

36608982R00101